The Christmas Tales

The third volume in
a collection of writings by

C.J.S. Hayward

C.J.S. Hayward Publications, Wheaton

1. Orthodox Eastern Church--fiction. 2. Orthodox Eastern Church--spirituality. 3. Orthodox Eastern Church--theology. 4. Time--theology. 5. Platonism. 6. Orthodox Eastern Church--humor. 7. Theology--humor.

ISBN 978-0-6151-9363-2

The reader is invited to visit CJSHayward.com.

Contents

1054 and All That

The Confused Person's Guide to Being Even More Confused About Orthodoxy

Eastern Orthodoxy is exactly like Roman Catholicism, except that it is Oriental and exotic. The Catholic Church split off from the Orthodox Church because the Orthodox would not accept the *filioque* clause, an anti-Arian shibboleth which offended the traditional Orthodox reverence for Constantine (a baptized Arian). The Orthodox Church is very wise because it has traditionally used the Julian Calendar to have an extra thirteen days to prepare and contemplate before each day. Each year, the Orthodox Church also rolls a die and holds Easter up to six weeks later than in the West, just to make things more confusing.

The Orthodox Church, sometimes called the Church of the Seven Ecumenical Councils, held seven ecumenical councils in response to controversies that arose. The main results were that the Church officially ruled out certain misunderstandings of Christ. The first council was the Council at Nicaea, modern day Nice, where Saint Nicholas of Myra and Lycia (our jolly old Saint Nick) boxed Arius on the ear. The Council at Nicaea rejected Aryanism, which teaches that Christ had blonde hair and blue eyes (a misunderstanding which is still prevalent in the land of blonde hair and blue ears). The other councils are really not that important, as they dealt with abtruse ancient controversies and don't have much to say about the modern and practical questions people struggle with today, such as whether Jesus was really tempted like us, or was just play-acting. The word "ecumenical" comes from the Greek οικουμενη, meaning the whole civilized world. Catholics and Orthodox disagree whether there are still being ecumenical councils; the Catholics, who are traditionally more universal and embracing, believe that a council without Orthodox bishops can still be ecumenical, while the Orthodox (considered by the Catholics to be schismatic) do not believe one can hold an ecumenical council without healing certain divisions, a task which faces any number of daunting obstacles, ranging from the Catholic Church's progressive Westernization to the Archbishop of Canterbury's demonstration that an Anglican can be a Druid. (If you find this confusing, don't worry. Most Orthodox don't understand it either.)

Understanding the Orthodox understanding of understanding is a point that is not often appreciated, partly because the syntax of "understanding the Orthodox understanding of understanding" is very confusing. The Orthodox believe, as Catholics still do on paper if not in practice, that we have a logos (from the Greek λογοσ, meaning the part of the mind we use to keep track of facts related to corporate logos), and a noose (from the Greek νουσ, meaning the part of the mind we use to grasp spiritual realities), and with typical ingenuity the Orthodox insist on using the noose for practical matters. The noose is very different from any Western understanding of mind, but if I explained it you wouldn't believe the claim that Orthodoxy is ordinary, concerned with the here and now, and not exotic in the way people assume. Some Orthodox, caught up in the Celtic culture boom, want to represent the noose with a stylized knot.

The words at the institution of Holy Communion, λαβετε φαγετε (literally, "Take, eat") have been misunderstood in the West (i.e. Catholics and Protestants) to mean "Take, understand." In the East, among Orthodox, people have insisted on preserving the apostolic meaning unchanged and have therefore reacted against the West and taken the text to mean, "Take, but do not understand." The Orthodox is free to say that the Eucharist is a symbol, on the understanding that this does not mean anything like the Western understanding of "just a symbol." The Orthodox is also equally free to claim that transsubstantiation occurs, on condition that "transsubstantiation" does not mean what the Catholic doctrine says it means.

Grace is like the sun in Orthodoxy: not only do we see it, but it allows us to see everything else. "Grace" characteristically means different things for Catholic, Orthodox, and Protestant; for Catholics "grace" is what we create by our works, for Orthodox "grace" is when God gives himself, and for Protestants "Grace" is a woman's name. Grace is behind works, sacraments, and everything else--food and drink, for that matter. Orthodox believe that God's grace rains down from Heaven, and because "He has established the *round* world so sure, it shall never be moved," God's grace then collects at the center of the earth.

Fully Orthodox believers may be divided into cradle Orthodox, who don't understand Orthodoxy very well and tend not to take it seriously, and convert Orthodox, who overdo *everything*. Orthodox are required to remain in communion with their bishops, which means community and a degree of submission to authority; people who fail to do this are called non-canonical, schismatic, etc. Non-canonical "Orthodox" are notorious for a rigid legalism in their interpretation of ancient canons. Canonical Orthodox take the matter much more lightly and often do not know the difference between a canon and a cannon.

There are many ranks of clergy, including (but not limited to) readers*, subdeacons, deacons, archdeacons, proper subdeacons, sub-sub-deacons, ostriches, priests, arch-priests, archimandrites, bishops, arch-bishops, bishops of the caves, metropolitans, patriarchs, prophets, ascetics, protons, neutrons, and Abednegons. There is a proper way of addressing each of these ranks, and it is traditional to embarrass your priest by not knowing how to address the higher ranks of clergy or (at your option) not being sure how to address *any* clergy.

    * Remember that Orthodoxy originated at a time when most people didn't know how to read and write, and Orthodoxy hasn't seen mass literacy as reason to change its practices. The positive way of stating this is that Orthodoxy, while incorporating the act of writing, preserves many of the attributes and the essential spirit of an oral tradition and culture, an achievement which may be appreciated in light of the anthropological observation that the opposite of "literate" is not "illiterate" but "oral". In other words, a Catholic is an Orthodox who can read.

    Orthodoxy has been blessed by many great theologians, including Saint Dionysius the Aereopagite, who was not Saint Dionysius the Aeropagite but another writer known as Saint Dionysius the Aeropagite, and Saint Maximus Confessor, who stalwartly resisted the heresy that Christ lacked a human will, and whose intricate analysis of will concluded that we have something called a "gnomic" will and Christ does not. Augustine is not revered nearly so much in the East, owing to the fact that he became a Christian and in fact a bishop without realizing he was supposed to stop being a Manichee. (This is why Augustine is considered the founder of American Catholicism.) The Orthodox consider the patristic era to be a golden age for theology; it ended in the ninth century and has produced a small number of patristic theologians since its close.

    In contrast to American individualism, the Orthodox Church talks about how when we come closer to Christ the more closely we resemble each other. This spirit of uniformity is demonstrated by her saints, who have been known to live on top of a pillar, make acts of public foolishness a form of spiritual discipline, or walk around after their deaths.

    Icons are called "windows of Heaven" and, apart from being an emblem of matter drawn into spiritual glory, provide a place where saints can look in and see how people like them were on earth. This is a humbling enough experience for the saints, so that they no longer have problems with pride.

    Please *do* ask why we aren't up to date enough to have women priests. Some Orthodox consider feminism to be an interesting spot of local color in our time and place, and at any rate the Orthodox will remember feminism as it remembers other challenges which lasted a mere century or two and which you probably haven't heard of. The Orthodox Church will continue discipling boys and girls, men and women, to be the men and women God created them to be, long after feminism is one more -ism that people of the future will learn about when they study the history of abandoned fashions. And besides, Orthodoxy *is* gender balanced. Cradle Orthodoxy is a woman thing, and convert Orthodoxy is a man thing.

It is an Orthodox principle that there should be one Orthodox Church in each country. That is why, if you are an American, you have your choice of Greek Orthodox, Russian Orthodox, Orthodox Church in America, Antiochian Orthodox...

Metania (μετανοια) is from meta (μετα) as in "metacognition" or "metaphysics", for a philosophical analysis of other things, and noia (νοια), which means mind but is not to be confused with the noose above. Hence "metania" means a philosophical discussion of how our minds should be functioning if we are Orthodox. This is very important in convert Orthodoxy; cradle Orthodox think converts miss metania completely. "Metania" also refers to an action performed with the body in worship, thus exemplifying the Orthodox penchant for conflating mind and body.

One closing word. Part of what distinguishes Orthodox theology is that it is no more systematic than the Church Fathers. In keeping with this tradition, this introduction is proudly disorganized.

Stephanos

The crown of Earth is the temple,
and the crown of the temple is Heaven.

Stephan ran to get away from his pesky sister--if nothing else he could at least outrun her!

Where to go?

One place seemed best, and his legs carried him to the chapel--or, better to say, the temple. The chapel was a building which seemed larger from the inside than the outside, and (though this is less remarkable than it sounds) it is shaped like an octagon on the outside and a cross on the inside.

Stephan slowed down to a walk. This place, so vast and open and full of light on the inside--a mystically hearted architect who read *The Timeless Way of Building* might have said that it breathed--and Stephan did not think of why he felt so much at home, but if he did he would have thought of the congregation worshipping with the skies and the seas, the rocks and the trees, and choir after choir of angels, and perhaps he would have thought of this place not only as a crown to earth but a room of Heaven.

What he was thinking of was the Icon that adorns the Icon stand, and for that matter adorns the whole temple. It had not only the Icons, but the relics of (from left to right) Saint Gregory of Nyssa, Saint John Chrysostom, and Saint Basil the Great. His mother had told Stephan that they were very old, and Stephan looked at her and said, "Older than email? Now *that* is old!" She closed her eyes, and when she opened them she smiled. "Older than email," she said, "and electric lights, and cars, and a great many of the kinds of things in our house, and our country, and..." her voice trailed off. He said, "Was it as old as King Arthur?" She said, "It is older than even the tale of King Arthur and his Knights of the Round Table."

As he had kissed the relics, he had begun to understand that what made them important was something deeper than their old age. But he could not say what.

But now he opened the doors to the temple, smelled the faint but fragrant smell of incense--*frankincense*--and was surprised to see another Icon on the stand. (Oh, wait, he thought. There were frequently other Icons.) The Icon was Saint Mary of Egypt. (This Icon did not have any relics.) He looked at the Icon, and began to look into it. What was her story? He remembered the part of her story he liked best--when, very far from being a saint at the beginning of her life, she came to a church and couldn't go in. An invisible force barred her, and a saint, the Mother of God, spoke to her through an Icon. Stephan vaguely remembered Father saying something about how it was also important how after years of fasting from everything but bread or vegetables, she was discovered but refused to go back to places that would still have been a temptation to her.

She was very gaunt, and yet that gauntness held fierce power. When he had looked into the Icon--or through it, as one looks through a window--he kissed her hand and looked at the royal doors, light doors with a kind of wooden mesh (it was beautiful) and a tower of three Icons each. The royal doors were at the center of the low, open wall that guarded the holy of holies within the temple, a special place crowned by the altar. The top two Icons told the place, not of the Annunciation **to** the Mother of God, but the Annunciation **of** the Mother of God. He looked into the pictures and saw the Annunciation **of** the Mother of God: not when the Archangel said, "Hail, O favored One! The Lord is with you," but when the Virgin listened and replied, "Behold the handmaiden of the Lord. Let it be done to me according to your word."

The spine of Eve's sin was snapped.

Death and Hell had already begun to crumble.

After looking through these pictures--it was not enough to say that he simply looked at them, though it was hard to explain why--he turned around and was absorbed into the Icon painted as a mural on the sloped ceiling that was now before him.

If that was the answer to Eve's sin, this was the answer to Adam's sin.

The Icon was an Icon the color of sunrise--or was it sunset? Then he saw something he hadn't seen before, even though this was one of his favorite Icons. It was an Icon of the Crucifixion, and he saw Christ at the center with rocks below--obedience in a garden of desolation had answered disobedience in a garden of delights--and beyond the rocks, the Holy City, and beyond the Holy City a sky with bands and whorls of light the color of sunrise. Now he saw for the first time that where Christ's body met the sky there was a band of purest light around it. Christ had a halp that was white at the center and orange and red at the sides--fitting for the Christ who passed through the earth like a flame.

The flame made him think of the God Who Cannot Be Pushed Around. This God sent his Son, who was also the One Who Cannot Be Pushed Around. In his teaching, in his friendship, in his healing the sick and raising the dead, every step he made was a step closer to this, the Cross. And yet he did this willingly.

Stephan turned, and for a moment was drawn to the mural to the right, which was also breathtakingly beautiful. Two women bore myrrh (the oil that newly chrismated Orthodox have just been anointed with) to perform a last service--the last service they could perform--to a dearly loved friend. And yet they found an empty tomb, and a majestic angel announcing news they would not have dared to hope: the Firstborn of the Dead entered death and death could not hold him. Its power had more than begun to crumble. But then Stephan turned back, almost sharply. Yes, this was glory. This was glory and majesty and beauty. But Stephan was looking for the beginning of triumph...

...and that was right there in the Icon the color of sunrise. The Cross in itself was the victory of the God Who Cannot Be Pushed Around. However much it cost him, he never let go of his plan or his grace. Christ knew he could call for more than twelve legions of angels--but he never did. He walked the path the Father set before him to the very end.

Stephan stood, his whole being transported to the foot of the Cross. However long he spent there he did not know, and I do not know either. He looked through the Icon, and saw--*tasted*--the full victory of the God Who Cannot Be Pushed Around.

When he did look away, it was in the Light of that God. Everything now bore that Light. He went over to the relics of the patron saints of his land, and though they were much newer than the relics of Saint Gregory of Nyssa, Saint John Chrysostom, and Saint Basil the Great, that didn't seem to matter. It was like dust from another world--precious grains of sand from Heaven--and the Icon of Saint Herman of Alaska and Saint Innocent holding up a tiny building was richly colorful--"like a rainbow that has grown up," he heard one of the grown-ups say.

Then he walked over to the Icon of Saint Ignatius of Antioch, holding a scroll that was open partway, with his letter to the Romans: "Let me be given to the wild beasts, for by their means I can attain to God. I am God's wheat, and I am being ground by the teeth of the beasts, so that I may an"--but here the quotation stopped, leaving him wondering. That Icon itself was one of several old-looking, yellowed Icons--though not nearly the oldest around--held in a deep, rich brown wooden frame carved with grapevines and bunches of grapes, as many things in that room were carved (though some had intricate interwoven knots). Stephan said, "I want to be a martyr just like you, Saint Ignatius. Pray for me."

Then he walked over to an Icon that was much smaller, but showed a man standing besides a rustic settlement with an outer wall and turrets and doors and buildings inside. It looked medieval to him, and he wished he could enter that world. It was darkened and yellowed and had a gold leaf sky, and something was written at the top, but he couldn't read it because it was in a very old language: Old Slavonic.

Right by that Icon was Saint Anthony, the father of all monastics. He had a piercing gaze, and Stephan had the feeling he needed to confess something--but he couldn't think of anything besides his bout with his sister, and she had been a pest. He looked away.

Stephan looked at the Icon on the left of the wall, and saw the prince, Saint Vladimir, with buildings and spires behind him that looked like they were having a party.

Then Stephan stood in front of the main Icon of the Mother of God holding God the Son, though he stood some distance back. The background was gold, and this drew him in a different way than the Icon of Saint Vladimir. This more than any other did not work like a photograph. (Or at least he was more aware of this now.) It might look odd to people who were just used to photographs, but you could say that a photograph was just a picture, but to say this was just a picture would show that you missed what kind of a picture you were looking at. But he had trouble thinking of how. He didn't so much sense that he was looking inot the Icon as that the Mother of God and the Son of God were looking at him. He didn't even think of the Icon being the Icon of the Incarnation and First Coming.

Then he looked at the Icon of the Last Judgment, where Christ the King and Lord and Judge returns holding a book of judgment, a book that is closed because there is nothing left to determine.

He thought intensely. The First Coming of Christ was in a stable, in a cave, and a single choir of angels sung his glory. The Second and Glorious Coming he will ride on the clouds, with legion on legion of angels with him. The First Coming was a mystery, one you could choose to disbelieve--as many people did. There will be no mistaking the Second Coming. In the First

Coming, a few knees bowed. In the Second Coming, every knee will bow, in Heaven and on earth and under the earth, and every tongue will confess that Jesus Christ is Lord, some in bliss and rapture and others in utter defeat. At the First Coming, a lone star in the sky heralded Christ's birth. At the Second Coming, the stars will fall to earth like overripe figs and the sky recede as a vanishing scroll.

What were those chilling, terrifying words of Christ? "Depart from me, you who are damned, into the eternal fire prepared for the Devil and his angels. For I was hungry and you gave me nothing to eat, thirsty and you gave me nothing to drink, sick and in prison and you did not visit me, lacking clothes and you did not give me the dignity of having clothes to wear." Then the condemned will say, "Where did we see you hungry and not feed you, or thirsty or sick or in prison and not take care of you?" And the King and Lord and Judge will say, "I most solemnly tell you, as much as you did not do it for the least of these brothers and sisters, you did not do it for me."

Stephan looked at the Icon and said, "I wish Dad would let me give money to beggars when I see..." Then his voice trailed off. The words didn't feel right in his mouth. He looked at the solemn love in the Icon, and then his mind was filled with the memory of his sister in tears.

He slowly backed down from the Icon, feeling the gaze of the King and Lord and Judge. He turned to almost run--he was in too holy of a place to run, and...

Something stopped him from leaving. After struggling inside, he looked around, and his eyes came to rest on the Icon of the Crucifixion that was the color of sunrise. Now he had not noticed them earlier this time, but he saw the Mother of God on one side and the beloved disciple on the earth. What had he just heard in church on Sunday? "Christ said to the beloved disciple, who is not here named because he is the image of every disciple, 'Behold your Mother,' and to his Mother, 'Behold your Son.' Listen to me very carefully. He did not say, 'Behold another man who is also your son,' but something much stranger and more powerful: 'Behold your Son,' because to be Orthodox is to become Christ." Stephan started to think, "Gold for kingship, incense for divinity, myrrh for suffering--these are Christ's gifts but he shares them with the Church, doesn't he?" He looked up, and then looked down.

"But I need to go and apologize for hurting my sister."
Then Christ's icon walked out the door.

Jobs for Theologians

HAFD University
Consolidated Department of Theology and Geology

Is looking for adjunct professors. The ideal candidate will possess excellent written and oral communication skills, have a strong teaching record, be flexible, and be open to exploring the relationship between igneous, sedimentary, and metapmorphic rocks as compared to faith, hope, and love as theological virtues.

If interested, please fax CV along with letter of application to (888) 555-1212 or visit our website at *http://hafd.edu.*

HAFD University
Department of Medieval Studies

Is looking for a full-time tenure track professor with interest in the high middle ages and theology from an elfin perspective; the ideal candidate will be fluent in relevant languages including Elvish, be able to convey what exactly the refinement of elfin culture means in theological discourse, and be comfortable lecturing outdoors under moonlight while wearing chainmail.

If interested, please fax CV along with letter of application to (888) 555-1212 or visit our website at *http://hafd.edu.*

HAFD University
Office of Internet Degrees

Is looking for adjunct professors and is scraping the bottom of the barrel. The ideal candidate will have an independent stream of income, a first-class PhD, and be excited to have a dead-end job while doing other people's gruntwork.

If interested, please fax CV along with letter of application to (888) 555-1212 or visit our website at *http://hafd.edu.*

HAFD University
Office of Ecumenical Relations

Is looking for theologians willing to study the Archdruid of Canterbury. The ideal candidate will have a thorough grounding in the classic Christian tradition as expressed in the Anglican branch of the Church in dialogue and synthesis with contemporary expressions of bardic and druidic lore.

If interested, please fax CV along with letter of application and a sprig of mistletoe to (888) 555-1212 or visit our website at *http://hafd.edu.*

HAFD University
Office of Newer Classics' Translations

Is looking for a scholar to produce a fresh translation of *Einfuhrung das Christentum*, a foundational *Grundkurs* by the Rev. Dr. Karl Rahner, SJ.

The ideal candidate will hold PhDs in disciplines including Systematic Theology, Philosophy with attention to philosophical logic and philosophy of science, German, English, Linguistics, Cognitive Science/Psychology with analogies drawn from Human-Computer Interaction, Education, and A Partridge in a Pear Tree; and will have done prior work making translations of Rahner into English that do not leave the reader wishing for further English translation.

If interested, please fax CV along with letter of application to (888) 555-1212 or visit our website at *http://hafd.edu*.

Plato: The Allegory of the...
Flickering Screen?

Socrates: And now, let me give an illustration to show how far
   our nature is enlightened or unenlightened:--Behold! a
   human being in a darkened den, who has a slack jaw
   towards only source of light in the den; this is where he has
   gravitated since his childhood, and though his legs and neck
   are not chained or restrained any way, yet he scarcely turns
   round his head. In front of him are images from faroff,
   projected onto a flickering screen. And others whom he
   cannot see, from behind their walls, control the images like
   marionette players manipulating puppets. And there are
   many people in such dens, some isolated one way, some
   another.

Glaucon: I see.

Socrates: And do you see, I said, the flickering screen showing
   men, and all sorts of vessels, and statues and collectible
   animals made of wood and stone and various materials, and
   all sorts of commercial products which appear on the
   screen? Some of them are talking, and there is rarely
   silence.

Glaucon: You have shown me a strange image, and they are
   strange prisoners.

Socrates: Much like us. And they see only their own images, or the images of one another, as they appear on the screen opposite them?

Glaucon: True, he said; how could they see anything but the images if they never chose to look anywhere else?

Socrates: And they would know nothing about a product they buy, except for what brand it is?

Glaucon: Yes.

Socrates: And if they were able to converse with one another, wouldn't they think that they were discussing what mattered?

Glaucon: Very true.

Socrates: And suppose further that the screen had sounds which came from its side, wouldn't they imagine that they were simply hearing what people said?

Glaucon: No question.

Socrates: To them, the truth would be literally nothing but those shadowy things we call the images.

Glaucon: That is certain.

Socrates: And now look again, and see what naturally happens next: the prisoners are released and are shown the truth. At first, when any of them is liberated and required to suddenly stand up and turn his neck around, and walk and look towards the light, he will suffer sharp pains; the glare will distress him, and he will be unable to see the realities of which in his former state he had seen the images; and then imagine someone saying to him, that what he saw before

was an illusion, but that now, when he is approaching nearer
to being and his eye is turned towards more real existence,
he has a clearer vision, -what will be his reply? And you
may further imagine that his instructor is asking him to
things, not as they are captured on the screen, but in living
color -will he not be perplexed? Won't he imagine that the
version which he used to see on the screen are better and
more real than the objects which are shown to him in real
life?

Glaucon: Far better.

Socrates: And if he is compelled to look straight at the light, will
he not have a pain in his eyes which will make him turn
away to take and take in the objects of vision which he can
see, and which he will conceive to be in reality clearer than
the things which are now being shown to him?

Glaucon: True, he now will.

Socrates: And suppose once more, that he is reluctantly dragged
up a steep and rugged ascent, and hindered in his self-
seeking until he's forced to think about someone besides
himself, is he not likely to be pained and irritated? He will
find that he cannot simply live life as he sees fit, and he will
not have even the illusion of finding comfort by living for
himself.

Glaucon: Not all in a moment, he said.

Socrates: He will require time and practice to grow accustomed
to the sight of the upper world. And first he will see the
billboards best, next the product lines he has seen
advertised, and then things which are not commodities; then
he will talk with adults and children, and will he know
greater joy in having services done to him, or will he prefer
to do something for someone else?

Glaucon: Certainly.

Socrates: Last of he will be able to search for the One who is greatest, reflected in each person on earth, but he will seek him for himself, and not in another; and he will live to contemplate him.

Glaucon: Certainly.

Socrates: He will then proceed to argue that this is he who gives the season and the years, and is the guardian of all that is in the visible world, and is absolutely the cause of all things which he and his fellows have been accustomed to behold?

Glaucon: Clearly, he said, his mind would be on God and his reasoning towards those things that come from him.

Socrates: And when he remembered his old habitation, and the wisdom of the den and his fellow-prisoners, do you not suppose that he would felicitate himself on the change, and pity them?

Glaucon: Certainly, he would.

Socrates: And if they were in the habit of conferring honours among themselves on those who were quickest to observe what was happening in the world of brands and what new features were marketed, and which followed after, and which were together; and who were therefore best able to draw conclusions as to the future, do you think that he would care for such honours and glories, or envy the possessors of them? Would he not say with Homer, "Better to be the poor servant of a poor master" than to reign as king of this Hell, and to endure anything, rather than think as they do and live after their manner?

Glaucon: Yes, he said, I think that he would rather suffer anything than entertain these false notions and live in this miserable manner.

Socrates: Imagine once more, I said, such an one coming suddenly out of the sun to be replaced in his old situation; would he not be certain to have his eyes full of darkness, and seem simply not to get it?

Glaucon: To be sure.

Socrates: And in conversations, and he had to compete in one-upsmanship of knowing the coolest brands with the prisoners who had never moved out of the den, while his sight was still weak, and before his eyes had become steady (and the time which would be needed to acquire this new habit of sight might be very considerable) would he not be ridiculous? Men would say of him that up he went with his eyes and down he came without them; and that it was better not even to think of ascending; and if any one tried to loose another and lead him up to the light, let them only catch the offender, and they would give him an extremely heavy cross to bear.

Glaucon: No question. Then is the saying, "In the land of the blind, the one eyed man is king," in fact false?

Socrates: In the land of the blind, the one-eyed man is crucified. Dear Glaucon, you may now add this entire allegory to the discussion around a matter; the den arranged around a flickering screen is deeply connected to the world of living to serve your pleasures, and you will not misapprehend me if you interpret the journey upwards to be the spiritual transformation which alike may happen in the monk keeping vigil or the mother caring for children, the ascent of the soul into the world of spiritual realities according to my poor belief, which, at your desire, I have expressed whether rightly or wrongly God knows. But, whether true or false, my opinion is that in the world of knowledge the Source of goodness appears last of all, and is seen only with an effort; and, when seen, is also inferred to be the universal author of all things beautiful and right, parent of light and of the lord of light in this visible world, and the immediate source of reason and truth in the intellectual; and that this is the power upon which he who would act rationally, either in public or private life must have his eye fixed.

Glaucon: I agree, he said, as far as I am able to understand you.

Two Decisive Moments

Readings from Scripture for the day this was proclaimed:

And when he returned to Caper'na-um after some days, it was reported that he was at home. And many were gathered together, so that there was no longer room for them, not even about the door; and he was preaching the word to them. And they came, bringing to him a paralytic carried by four men. And when they could not get near him because of the crowd, they removed the roof above him; and when they had made an opening, they let down the pallet on which the paralytic lay. And when Jesus saw their faith, he said to the paralytic, "My son, your sins are forgiven."

Now some of the scribes were sitting there, questioning in their hearts, "Why does this man speak thus? It is blasphemy! Who can forgive sins but God alone?"

And immediately Jesus, perceiving in his spirit that they thus questioned within themselves, said to them, "Why do you question thus in your hearts? Which is easier, to say to the paralytic, `Your sins are forgiven,' or to say, `Rise, take up your pallet and walk'? But that you may know that the Son of man has authority on earth to forgive sins" -- he said to the paralytic -- "I say to you, rise, take up your pallet and go home."

And he rose, and immediately took up the pallet and went out before them all; so that they were all amazed and glorified God, saying, "We never saw anything like this!"

Mark 2:1-12, RSV

And, "Thou, Lord, didst found the earth in the beginning, and the heavens are the work of thy hands; they will perish, but thou remainest; they will all grow old like a garment, like a mantle thou wilt roll them up, and they will be changed. But thou art the same, and thy years will never end."

But to what angel has he ever said, "Sit at my right hand, till I make thy enemies a stool for thy feet"? Are they not all ministering spirits sent forth to serve, for the sake of those who are to obtain salvation?

Therefore we must pay the closer attention to what we have heard, lest we drift away from it. For if the message declared by angels was valid and every transgression or disobedience received a just retribution, how shall we escape if we neglect such a great salvation? It was declared at first by the Lord, and it was attested to us by those who heard him...

Hebrews 1:10-2:3, RSV

In the name of the Father, and of the Son, and of the Holy Ghost. Amen.

There is a classic Monty Python "game show": the moderator asks one of the contestants the second question: "In what year did Coventry City last win the English Cup?" The contestant looks at him with a blank stare, and then he opens the question up to the other contestants: "Anyone? In what year did Coventry City last win the English Cup?" And there is dead silence, until the moderator says, "Now, I'm not surprised that none of you got that. It is in fact a trick question. Coventry City has *never* won the English Cup."

I'd like to dig into another trick question: "When was the

world created: 13.7 billion years ago, or about six thousand years ago?" The answer in fact is "Neither," but it takes some explaining to get to the point of realizing that the world was created 3:00 PM, March 25, 28 AD.

Adam fell and dragged down the whole realm of nature. God had and has every authority to repudiate Adam, to destroy him, but in fact God did something different. He called Noah, Abraham, Moses, and Elijah, and in the fullness of time he didn't just call a prophet; he sent his Son to become a prophet and more.

It's possible to say something that means more than you realize. Caiaphas, the high priest, did this when he said, "It is better that one man be killed than that the whole nation perish." (John 11:50) This also happened when Pilate sent Christ out, flogged, clothed in a purple robe, and said, "*Behold the man!*"

What does this mean? It means more than Pilate could have possibly dreamed of, and "Adam" means "man": *Behold the man! Behold Adam, but not the Adam who sinned against God and dragged down the Creation in his rebellion, but the second Adam, the new Adam, the last Adam, who obeyed God and exalted the whole Creation in his rising. Behold the man, Adam as he was meant to be. Behold the New Adam who is even now transforming the Old Adam's failure into glory!*

Behold the man! Behold the first-born of the dead. Behold, as in the icon of the Resurrection, the man who descends to reach Adam and Eve and raise them up in his ascent. Behold the man who will enter the realm of the dead and forever crush death's power to keep people down.

An icon of the Resurrection.

Behold the man and behold the firstborn of many brothers!
You may know the great chapter on faith, chapter 11 of the book
of Hebrews, and it is with good reason one of the most-loved
chapters in the Bible, but it is not the only thing in Hebrews. The
book of Hebrews looks at things people were caught up in, from
the glory of angels to sacrifices and the Mosaic Law, and
underscores how much more the Son excels above them. A little

before the passage we read above, we see, "To which of the angels did he ever say, 'You are my son; today I have begotten you'?" (Hebrews 1:5) And yet in John's prologue we read, "To those who received him and believed in his name, he gave the authority to become the children of God." (John 1:9) We also read today, "To which of the angels did he ever say, 'Sit at my right hand until I have made your enemies a footstool under your feet?'" (Hebrews 1:13) And yet Paul encourages us: "The God of peace will shortly crush Satan under your feet," (Romans 16:20) and elsewhere asks bickering Christians, "Do you not know that we will judge angels?" (I Corinthians 6:3) *Behold the man! Behold the firstborn of many brothers, the Son of God who became a man so that men might become the Sons of God. Behold the One who became what we are that we might by grace become what he is. Behold the supreme exemplar of what it means to be Christian.*

Behold the man and behold the first-born of all Creation, through whom and by whom all things were made! Behold the Uncreated Son of God who has entered the Creation and forever transformed what it means to be a creature! Behold the Saviour of the whole Creation, the Victor who will return to Heaven bearing as trophies not merely his transfigured saints but the whole Creation! Behold the One by whom and through whom all things were created! Behold the man!

Pontius Pilate spoke words that were deeper than he could have **possibly** imagined. And Christ continued walking the fateful journey before him, continued walking to the place of the Skull, Golgotha, and finally struggled to breathe, his arms stretched out as far as love would go, and barely gasped out, "It is finished."

Then and there, the entire work of Creation, which we read about from Genesis onwards, was *complete*. There and no other place the world was created, at 3:00 PM, March 25, 28 AD. *Then* the world was created.

That is a decisive moment, but decisive moments are not some kind of special exception to Christian life. Christian history and the Christian spiritual walk alike take their pace from decisive moments. I would like to look at the decisive moment in the Gospel reading.

In that reading, the people who have gathered to listen to Jesus went beyond a "standing room only" crowd to being so packed you couldn't get near the door. Some very faithful friends of a paralytic did the only thing they could have done. They climbed on the roof and started digging through it. I suspect that the homeowner didn't like the idea. But they dug in, and lowered him, hoping this teacher will heal him.

Jesus saw *their* faith and said, "Your sins are forgiven." And people were shocked--there was a very good reason for this! If I have two friends, and one owes the other money, I can't tell the first one, "Your debt is forgiven. It's wiped clean." *That's not my place.* Sin is not a debt, or a crime, or even a disease. *It's worse.* And Christ told a man who owed an infinite debt to God that his slate was wiped clean and his sins were forgiven. And the reason people were saying, "This man blasphemes! Who can forgive sins but God alone?" was that they understood exactly how significant it was for Jesus to say, "Your sins are forgiven." Maybe they failed to recognize Christ as God (it is very rare that anyone but the demons identified him as the Son of God), but they were absolutely right when they said that Jesus was saying something that only God had the authority to say.

They were murmuring, and Christ knew why. So he asked them, "Which is easier: to say, 'Your sins are forgiven,' or to say, 'Arise. Take up your mat and walk.'" Everybody knew the answer, that forgiving sins was an infinitely weightier matter, but Jesus was about to give a lesser demonstration of the exact same authority by which he said, "Your sins are forgiven." He said to the paralytic, "Arise. Take up your mat and walk." And the paralytic did exactly that.

That is authority. That is the authority that commands the blind to gaze on the light of the Transfiguration, the deaf to listen to the song of angels, the mute to sing with God's angels, the lame to dance for joy, and what is greater than all of these, command you and me, sinners, to be freed from our sins.

Great and rare as the restoration of one paralytic may be, everybody knew that that was less important than the forgiveness of his sins. The story of that healing is a decisive moment.

But it's not the only decisive moment, and there is another decisive moment that may be much less rare, much less something we want to write home about, but is profoundly important, especially in Lent. I am talking about repentance.

When the Holy Spirit convicts me of my sin, there are two responses I give, both of which I ought to be ashamed of. The first response is to tell God that he doesn't know what he's talking about. Now of course I am not blunt enough to tell God, "You don't know what you're doing." (Perhaps it would be better if I did.) What I say instead is something like, "I can see where you're coming from, and I can see that you have a point. But I've given it a little thought and I'd like you to consider a suggestion that is much better for everyone involved. Would you consider this consolation prize?" Now again, perhaps it would be better if I were honest enough to simply tell God, "You don't know what you're doing." Not only is it not good that I do that, but it is spurning the grace of God.

When a mother takes a knife or a sharp pair of scissors from a little boy, this is not because the mother wants a pair of scissors and is too lazy or inconsiderate to go get her own pair: her motivation is entirely for the child's welfare. God doesn't need our repentance or our sin. When he commands us through his Spirit to let go of our sin, is this for our sake or for his need? It is entirely for our own benefit, and not something God was lacking, that we are commanded to repent from sin. And this has a deeper implication. If God convicts us from our sin and asks our surrender to him in the unconditional surrender for repentance, then that is how we will be healed from our sin: it is the best medicine chosen by the Great Physician, *and it is out of his mercy that the Great Physician refuses all of our consolation prizes that will cut us off from his healing love*. Repentance is terrifying at times; it is letting go of the one thing we least want to give over to God, and it is only once we have let go that our eyes are opened and we realize, "I was holding on to a piece of Hell!" The more we understand repentance the more we understand that it is a decisive moment when God is at work.

The second response I give to the Holy Spirit is even more an affront to the decisive *now* in which the Lord meets me. I say, "Well, I think you're right, and I need to repent of it, only now isn't the best time for me. I'd like to deal with it at another time." Here, also, things might be better if I were at least honest enough to acknowledge I was telling God, "Your timing is far from perfect." God lives outside of time, and yet he has all the time there is. There is never reason for him to say with a sheepish grin, "I know this really isn't the best time for you, but I only have two minutes right now, and I'm going to ask for you to deal with this now even though this isn't the best time." When he comes and tells us to repent, now, the reason for that is not that some point later on we may feel more like repenting and that is a better time; the reason is that by the time I am struggling against God's Spirit I have already entered the decisive moment when I can choose either to be cleansed and freed of my sin, or keep on fumbling for the snooze button while God tells me, "Enough sleep! It is time for you to arise!"

Let us repent, in the name of the Father, and of the Son, and of the Holy Ghost. Amen.

A Glimpse into Eastern Orthodoxy

Introduction

Do children and adults understand each other? To some degree, and if many adults have lost touch with childhood, there are some who understand childhood very well. But when I was a child, I wanted to write a book about things adults don't understand about children. (I have since forgotten with what I wanted to write.) There is a gulf. A father can read a <u>Calvin and Hobbes</u> strip, and his little girl can ask what's funny, and the father is in a pickle. It's not that he doesn't want to explain it, and he may be able to explain the humor to another adult, but all of those explanations fail with his daughter. Children often believe that there's a big secret the adult conspiracy is refusing to tell them. And the adult who is trying to get a child to "be serious" by setting aside "make believe" and dealing with what is "real" is like someone who wears a raincoat to the shower. The things that go without saying as part of being serious are in many cases not part of childhood's landscape.

In this sense, children understand each other. This understanding is compatible with friendship, liking, hating, being aloof, and several other things, but there are certain things that go without saying, and the things that go without saying are shared. Two young children will have a world where the difference between "real" and "imaginary" is not very important, where they have no power and adults laugh at things the children don't understand, and where the world is full of wonder. And in that sense two children can understand each other even if they don't know each other's heroes, favorite ways to play, and so on and so forth. And adults likewise understand things that can normally be taken for granted among adults.

Before suggesting that Western Christianity (in other words, Catholic and Protestant Christianity) is best understood in continuity with the West, I would like to explain what I mean. There are a good many Catholics and Protestants who try to be critical towards Western culture, and who do not accept uncritically what is in vogue. I know several Western Christians who tried to live counterculturally and not accept sour things in Western culture; I was such a Western Christian myself. So is it fair to talk about the continuity between Western Christianity and the West?

There is a common Western tendency to criticize common Western tendencies. I've seen Christians eager to criticize Western tendencies. I've also seen liberals who were not Christian eagerly criticize common Western tendencies. For that matter, I don't remember ever hearing someone use the term "common Western tendency" in a flattering way, even though the West is home to many great cultural triumphs (as well as problems). Criticizing "Western tendencies" is a Western thing to do. Taking a dim view of the culture that raised you is a Western thing to do. Working to create a counterculture is a Western thing to do. The focus of this article is not to rebut the West but to explain the East and describe things Western Christians may not know to look for. The Orthodox classics do not try to be Christian by making unflattering remarks about "common Western tendencies." For reasons that I will elaborate, I know that there are countercultural Western Christians who strive to construct or reconstruct a Christian culture that is very different from the Western mainstream (I was such a countercultural Western Christian), and I still consider their continuities with the West to be significant. More on that later.

This article explores the suggestion that **Eastern**

(Orthodox) Christianity is best understood in continuity with the East, and Western (Catholic and Protestant) Christianity is best understood in continuity with the West. There are of course continuities between Eastern and Western Christianity. But they usually aren't the point where Western Christians do not understand Orthodox. There are important ways that a Western Christian understands an Eastern Christian and members of (other) Eastern religions don't. There are also important ways that members of (mostly) Eastern religions understand each other. **The purpose of this article is to explain things that the East naturally understands about Orthodoxy**, not to explain everything important about Orthodoxy. The understanding between Orthodox, Hindus, Muslims, Orthodox Jews, Buddhists, and many less well known religions is of this kind. And so is understanding within the West, but East and West are different as children and adults are different--not because one is more mature than the other (each can see the other as childish), but because there is a gulf. The understanding isn't a matter of how many details you know, or agreement on important matters. For that matter, it's not even a matter of civil disagreement. Understanding another religion is perfectly consistent with fighting religious wars. But there is a gulf that is rarely bridged, and I am trying to bring a spark of understanding of the gulf. I am trying to explain what is shared that Westerns, even Western Christians, need to have explained. And I will be looking at both East and West, at both worlds.

This article is partly Eastern and partly Western, and doesn't completely belong to either world. It's meant to give explanations a Westerner would recognize, while addressing important things that a Westerner might not think to ask about. I was raised an evangelical, and I am a relatively recent convert to Eastern Orthodoxy. This means that for better or worse I have a foot in both worlds. I hope to use this position to build a bridge.

The Most Important Thing Is

"Article on understanding Orthodoxy" is a dread oxymoron, a red flag like the phrase "committee to revitalize," or for that matter a thick commentary on Ecclesiastes 6:11: "The more the words, the less the meaning, and how does that profit anyone?" (NIV)

Orthodoxy is something you understand by doing. If you want to learn to swim, you get in the water with someone who can show you how to swim. So the first thing an article on understanding Orthodoxy can say is that you can't understand Orthodoxy by reading an article on understanding Orthodoxy. You can understand it by visiting a parish and seeing how we worship, and maybe participating. A book can be a useful tour guide that can help you keep your eyes open for what to see at a historic site, but it cannot substitute for visiting the site yourself. The first thing to do is, if you know someone Orthodox, ask, "May I join you at church?" Orthodoxy is a live community, and the way to understand it is to interact with the community. If you don't have that live connection, you can <u>search online for a nearby parish</u>. Some parishes (churches) are warmer than others. There are some parishes that unfortunately aren't welcoming. If a church doesn't have a sign out in front, that may be a warning. But there are many churches that are welcoming. And don't worry if everybody seems to be doing things that you don't understand. There is a great deal of freedom in Orthodoxy, and apart from receiving communion you should be welcome to do (or not do) anything people are doing. Sometimes you will see different members of the faithful doing different things, walking around, entering, leaving. This is because of the freedom in Orthodox worship and a grand tradition of not sticking your nose in what other people are doing. When I first visited my present parish, well before I became Orthodox, I was self-conscious about following what other people were doing and sticking out. In the time that I've been Orthodox, I realized that there was no need to be self-conscious, and in fact no one cared that I wasn't acting like everyone else.

So make a note in your planner, or call a friend who's

Orthodox. Decide exactly when you will make that contact, and do what you need to do to get that in your planner. Actually visiting the site is infinitely more valuable than reading a guidebook about it.

Symbol and Nominalism

Before explaining what symbol is in the East, I would like to talk about what has happened in the West. Symbol in the West used to be close to what it was in the East--like two trees standing tall. Then something called *nominalism* came along, and cut down the Western tree, leaving a stump of a once great tree. Nominalism is a good part of what has defined the West.

Nominalism was one side in a Western medieval debate, and it was called the "modern way." The debate was whether categories of things were something real that existed before things and before our minds, or whether categories are things we construct after the fact. What people used to believe, and what the nominalists' opponents believed, was that a lot more things were real than the nominalists acknowledged. Their opponents looked at the structures we perceive and said, "It's out there," and the nominalists said "No, it only exists in your head." Nominalism was an axe for cutting down most of what people sensed about the world around us. In its extreme form nominalism says that brute fact is all that exists; if it's not a brute fact, it can only exist in people's heads. Some scholars will recognize that as a postmodern distinction; nominalism was something that flowered in modernism and bore fruit in postmodernism. At one stage, nominalism defined modernism and the Enlightenment, while at a later stage, people were more consistent and became postmodern.

Another thing that nominalism did was to cut apart the thing that represents and the thing that is represented in a symbol. **Nominalism is the disenchantment of the entire universe.** Nominalism is a disenchanting force that says, "If you can't touch it, it can only be in your head," and the place of symbol was changed from what it once was. Symbol wasn't the only casualty, but it was one of the casualties.

Imagine two very different surfaces, like the surface of the ground. The first surface, Orthodoxy, is rich in connections, layers, and colors. Imagine that the first surface is textured, like the surface of the earth, while there are not only buildings but great arcs connecting one part to another so that what is present in one place is present in another. A symbol is an arc of this kind, and symbol is not something externally added to reality; it is something basic to what reality is, so that the surface is in fact richer than just a surface and is as connected as a web. If there is something in you that responds to beauty in the surface, or to ways it has become ugly, that is because something inside you is resonating with something out there.

Now imagine another picture, of a surface that is flat and grey, where there is no real order, and any structures and connections you see are only ways of lumping things together inside your head. You can read things on to it; you can imagine structures in its randomness and pretend any two parts are linked; because it has no order, you can project any kind of structure or connection you want, even if this freedom means it is only your particular fantasy. If you find it to be drab and empty, that is a private emotional reaction that says nothing interesting about the drab and empty world, in particular not that it is failing to be in some way colorful like it "should" be. "Should" has no meaning beyond something about our private psychology.

If you imagine these two surfaces--one of them structured, many-layered, colorful, and possessing a veritable web of connecting arcs (symbols), and the other one having only a single grey layer and no connections--you have the difference between what Orthodoxy believes and where nominalism leads. Few people believe nominalism in a pure form; I don't even know if it is *possible* to believe nominalism in a few form. Nominalism is more a way of decaying than a fixed system of ideas. Part of what has shaped Western Christianity is the influence of nominalism as the disenchantment of the entire universe. Nominalism disenchants the treasure of a world of spiritual resonance, where symbol and memory have a rich meaning, where a great many things are not private psychological phenomena but something that is attuned to the world as a whole, as much as a radio picks up music because someone is broadcasting the music it picks up.

What was before nominalism in the West, and what is the place of symbol in Orthodoxy now? Christ is a symbol of God, and he is a symbol in the fullest possible sense. How? Christ is not a miniature separate copy of God, which is what a symbol often is in the West. Christ is fully united with God: "I and the Father are One." God is fundamentally beyond our world; "No man can see God and live." But "in Christ the fullness of God lives in a body." And if you have seen Christ, you have seen the Father. Christ visibly expresses the Father's hidden reality.

The image of God, in which we were all created, does not mean that we are detached miniature copies of God. What it means is that we, in our inmost being, are fundamentally connected to God. It means that we were created to participate in God's reality, and that something of God lives in us. It means that every breath we breathe is the breath of God. It means that we are to reign as God's delegates, the moving wonders who manifest God in ruling his visible world.

As an aside, symbol is one important kind of connection that makes things really present, but it's not the only one. Memory is not understood as a psychological phenomenon inside the confines of a person's head; to remember something is to make something really present. "This do in rememberance of me" is not primarily about us having thoughts in our heads about Christ, just as saying "Please assemble this cabinet" is not primarily about us seeing and touching tools and cabinet pieces. Saying "Please assemble this cabinet" may include seeing and touching what needs to be assembled, but the focus is to bring about a fully assembled cabinet which not just something in our minds. When Christ said "This do in rememberance of me", he wasn't just talking about a psychological phenomenon, however much that may be necessary for remembering; he was telling us to make him really present and be open to his presence, and he isn't present "just" in our thinking any more than a working cabinet is "just" a set of sensations we had in the course of assembling it. And the idea of "This do in rememberance of me" goes hand in hand with Holy Communion being a symbol in the fullest possible sense: the bread and wine represent the body and blood of Christ. The bread and wine embodies the body and blood of Christ. The bread and wine *are* the body and blood of Christ. All of these are tied together.

Amomg these symbols, a reader may be surprised about one kind of symbol I haven't mentioned: the icon. Icons are something I tried to overlook to get to the good parts of Orthodoxy; it took a while for me to recognize how much icons *are* one of the good parts of Orthodoxy. Icons are in fact key to understanding Orthodoxy.

When one bishop is giving a speech, sometimes he will hold up a picture, of a traffic intersection (or something else obviously secular), and then say, "In Greece, this is an icon. It's not a holy icon, but it's an icon."

Part of what icons are in the East is easier to understand in light of what happened to icons in the West, not only religious artwork but painting as a whole. What happens if you ask an art historian to tell the story of Western art after the Middle Ages, roughly from the Renaissance to the Neo-classicists?

The story that is usually told is a story of Western art growing from crude and inaccurate depictions to paintings that were almost like photographs. It is a story of progress and advancement.

Orthodoxy can see something else in the story. Western art became photorealistic, not because they progressed from something inferior, but because their understanding of symbol had disintegrated.

If a picture is real to you as a symbol, then you don't have to strive too hard to "accomplish" the picture, in the same sense that someone who has never gotten in trouble with alcohol doesn't have to make an unprovoked lecture on why he doesn't have a drinking problem. People who use alcohol responsibly rarely feel the need to prove that they don't have a drinking problem; it's someone who has a drinking problem who feels the need to make sure you know that his drinking is under control. People who don't have a problem don't feel the need to defend themselves, and artists and publics who haven't lost symbols don't feel a need to cram in photorealism. When Renaissance artists inaccurately portrayed the place of Christ's birth as having a grid of rectangular tiles, they were cramming in photorealism. It wasn't even that they thought they needed photorealism to make a legitimate picture. They went beyond that need to make the picture an opportunity to demonstrate photorealism, whether or not the photorealism really belonged there. From an Orthodox perspective the problem is not the historical inaccuracy of saying that Christ was born in a room with a tiled floor instead of a cave. The anachronism isn't that big of a deal. From an Orthodox perspective the problem is that, instead of making a symbol the way people do when they really believe in symbol, people were making pictures the way people do when the pictures are unreal to them as symbols. The artists went for broke and pushed the envelope on photorealism because the West had lost something much more important than photorealism.

Good Orthodox icons don't even pretend to be photorealistic, but this is not simply because Orthodox iconography has failed to learn from Western perspective. As it turns out, Orthodox icons use a reverse perspective that is designed to include the viewer in the picture. Someone who has become a part of the tradition is drawn into the picture, and in that sense an icon is like a door, even if it's more common to call icons "windows of Heaven." But it's not helpful to simply say "Icons don't use Renaissance perspective, but reverse perspective that includes the viewer," because even if the reverse perspective is there, reverse perspective is simply not the point. There are some iconographers who are excellent artists, and artistry does matter, but the point of an icon is to have something more than artistry, as much as the point of visiting a friend is more than seeing the scenery along the way, even if the scenery is quite beautiful and adds to the pleasure of a visit. Cramming in photorealism is a way of making more involved excursions and dredging up more exotic or historic or whatever destinations that go well beyond a scenic route, after you have lost the ability to visit a friend. The Western claim is "Look at how much more extravagant and novel my trip are than driving along the same roads to see a friend!"--and the Orthodox response shows a different set of priorities: "Look how lonely you are now that you no longer visit friends!"

The point is that an icon, being a symbol, is connected to the person represented. It is probably not an accident that in the Reformation, the most iconoclastic people were those in whom the concept of symbol as spiritual connection had completely disintegrated. When I was a Protestant, the plainest sanctuaries I saw were the sanctuaries belonging to people who disbelieved in symbols as spiritual connections. If a symbol is not spiritually connected, then reverence to an icon is inappropriate reverence to a piece of wood; Orthodox believe that reverence to an icon passes through to the saint depicted in part because of the connection that is real to them.

There are other things to discuss about icons. Here I want to talk about them as symbols, and symbols in an Orthodox picture-- the mental image I drew above that has a web of interconnections, has both spiritual and material layers, and is very different from the (almost empty) nominalist picture. A lot of people who try to understand icons are trying to fit the Orthodox icon into the nominalist picture, or at least a picture where part of the Orthodox framework is replaced with something more nominalist. I want to return to icons later, after some comparisons.

Compare and Contrast

How is Orthodoxy different from Western Christianity? I would like to answer, focusing on evangelical Christianity in my treatment of Western Christianity but referring to Catholicism. I don't believe evangelical Christianity is the only real version of Western Christianity, but it is the middle of the (Western) road.

From an Orthodox perspective, "Catholic," "evangelical," and "mainline" (or, if you prefer an alternative to "mainline," you can say "oldline," or "sideline," or "flatline") represent three degrees of being Western, much as "rare," "medium," and "well done" denote three degrees of a steak being cooked. There are important differences, but there is also something that's the same. Catholicism is like a rare steak, is almost raw in some parts and almost well done in others. A Catholic may be almost Orthodox (certainly a Catholic is not discouraged from trying to be almost Orthodox), and there are a lot of Catholics who believe that Vatican II says that the Reformers were right about everything (or something pretty close to that).

Catholics tend to be sensitive to the differences to Catholic and Protestant (even if they choose not to pay enough attention to those differences). Yet it is common for Catholics to believe that Catholics and Orthodox only differ in the addition of "and the Son" to a creed. Saying that's the only difference between Catholicism and Orthodoxy is like saying that the difference between the Bible and the Quran is only that "Bible" was a French word for "book" and "Quran" is, with remarkable similarity, an Arabic word that can mean "book." Catholic priests will tell you that Catholics and Orthodox believe almost exactly the same thing, and this is because Catholics know how they are different from Protestants but don't know where their differences with Orthodox lie. The Reformation took a lot of trends in Catholicism and pushed them much further, but the problem isn't just that the Reformers pushed them further. The problem is that the trends became a part of Catholicism in the first place. To Catholic readers who have been told that Catholicism is almost the same as Orthodoxy and the two should be joined together--I understand why you believe that and it is what one would expect the Catholic tradition to say. But to the Orthodox that is like saying that the Quran is of a piece with the Bible. You're looking in the wrong place for the differences between the Bible and the Quran when you try to reconcile them by pointing out that "Bible" and "Quran" both mean book in influental languages. Not only do the differences lie elsewhere, they are far, far deeper.

Western Christianity	**Orthodoxy**
Sin is understood as essentially crime, and the remedy to sin provided by Christ is understood as being cleared for the guilt of a crime. Hence in *Pilgrim's Progress*, for instance, there are elaborations designed to convince you that your crimes (sins) are great, and that you cannot ever clear yourself of these crimes (sins), but Bunyan does not seem to even see the question of whether sin and the consequence of sin are like anything besides crime and criminal guilt.	Sin is understood as spiritual disease, and the remedy to sin provided by Christ is understood as healing. The Eucharist is "for the healing of soul and body," and as the Great Physician Christ is concerned for both spiritual disease and physical disease, and drawing people into the divine life that he gives.
The reformation created mass literacy so that everyone could read the Bible. As a culture, it is heavily oriented towards written text. Someone said after visiting an Orthodox Church that it was the only church he'd been to	If evangelicalism is essentially a written culture, then in keeping with the observation that the opposite of a "literate" culture is not "illiterate" but "oral," Orthodoxy has the attributes of an oral tradition. Many of its members can read and write, but writing has different implications.

that didn't offer him printed material. At least for Protestant churches, a visitor is offered some kind of paper documents; there is a bulletin that is passed out; one of my friends had been a member of church where people said "No creed but Christ!" (which he was quick to point out, *is a creed*), and then asked him to sign a sixty page doctrinal statement.	It's the difference between a natural environment that includes some things people have created (a campsite) and a basically artificial environment (a laboratory). At the parish where I was accepted into the Orthodox Church, there was no literature rack and no stack of booklets for you to follow along the service. Even where those booklets are offered, incidentally, I prefer to participate without reading what is being said--I think it's not just economic reasons that the main historic way for Orthodox to follow along a service doesn't depend on reading. Part of an oral tradition means things that are alive, things that are passed on that have a different basic character to what can be preserved in a text. This is present in Western Christianity, but it is more pronounced in Orthodoxy.
The written character of the culture is focused on Scripture. It is expected, especially among Evangelicals, that if your faith is strong, you will read Scripture privately. Catholics and some	Scripture is the crowning jewel of Tradition. Scripture is not something understood apart from Tradition; Scripture is something alive, something dynamically maintained by Tradition and something inspired not only in that the Spirit inspired ancient

Protestants do not believe Scripture has sole authority; Catholics assert the authority of Tradition alongside Scripture ("Scripture and Tradition"), and different Protestant groups have different solutions to the problem of how to balance the authority of Scripture and tradition.

words but in that he speaks today to people who can listen to him. And Scripture is at its fullest, not read privately, but when proclaimed in Church.

One Orthodox priest tells people, "Reading Scripture privately is the second most spiritually dangerous thing you can do. All sorts of temptations will flare up, you'll be assailed by doubts, and the Devil will whisper into your ear all these heretical 'insights' about the text. It is an extraordinarily dangerous thing to do."

Some people are intimidated, wonder if they should really be reading the Bible privately, and ask timidly, "Well, I should reconsider reading the Bible privately. But one question. What's the *most* dangerous thing you can do spiritually?"

"Not reading the Bible privately."

There is a set of important questions, "What part of the person do we know with?" "What is knowledge?" "How can knowledge be built in another person?" Let me start with some secular answers:

I'd like to answer the same basic questions as I outlined to the left:

What part of the person do we know with? At least in matters of faith, we know with something that could be called "spirit" or "mind," a part of us that is practical (the knowing we have

What part of the person do we know with? We know with the mind, which is what is studied by the secular discipline of cognitive psychology. One big example is the part of us that reasons.

What is knowledge? Knowledge is having true mental representations that correspond to the world. It is the sort of thing we acquire from books.

How can knowledge be built in another person? Knowledge is built, to speak crudely, by opening the head and dumping something in. Now of course we need words/numbers/pictures to do this, but you teach by a classroom or a book.

Now this is a purification of something that is mixed in any Western Christian. It doesn't even represent postmoderns well; in fact, it describes something postmoderns are trying to get away from. But admitting all these things, when something becomes real to us). This part of the person thinks precisely because it is the center of where we meet God. It is the part of us we use to pray and worship. It is part of us that is connected with God and can *only* be understood with reference to God.

What is knowledge? Knowledge is when you participate in something, when you drink it in, when you relate to it. Someone's talked about the difference between knowing facts about your wife, and knowing your wife. The West uses the first kind of knowledge as the heart of its picture of knowledge. Orthodoxy uses the second.

It is normally vain for a person to say, "To know me is to love me." But there is another reason why someone might say that. To know anything is to love it. To know any person is to love that person because knowledge is connected to love.

How can knowledge be built in another person? Knowledge works from the outside in. The reason the first chapter after the introduction asked you to visit Orthodox worship is that that is

there is an element of the above answers in how Western Christians understand knowledge. Many Western Christians do not purely believe these answers, but they do believe something mixed with them.	how one comes to understand Orthodoxy. We don't believe in trying to open the head and dump in knowledge. You can't gain knowledge of Orthodoxy that way. You might be able to learn some of the garments surrounding Orthodoxy, but not the spirit itself. The point of asking you to visit Orthodox worship is that that's not something important that needs to be added to learning about Orthodoxy. It *is* learning about Orthodoxy. By the way, the same kind of thing is true of evangelicalism, even if people are less aware of it. Evangelicalism can never be understood as a system of ideas. An evangelical might only be aware of the ideas to be known, but that can only happen if the participation-based knowledge of the evangelical walk, in other words the Orthodox kind of knowledge, is in place.
I'd like to look at one more specific kind of knowledge, theology. In the West, theology is an academic discipline, and used to be called the queen of the sciences.	It took me a long time to make head or tail of my deacon's insistence, "Theology is not philosophy whose subject-matter is God," or of the ancient saying, "A theologian is one who prays and one who prays is a

Theology is a system of ideas, much like philosophy, and every other kind of theology is a branch of systematic theology.

theologian." But that was because I was trying to fit them into my Western understanding of theology tightly tied to a philosophy.

Theology is not the queen of sciences because it is not a science, and only with reservations can it be called an academic discipline. Calling theology an academic discipline is like calling karate an academic discipline (because you can take classes in both at college). Academic theology has a place, and in fact I intend to study academic theology, but the real heart of theology is not in the academy, but in the Church at prayer.

Theology is knowledge. More specifically, it is mystical or spiritual knowledge. It is knowing with the part of you that prays, and that is why Orthodox still say, "A theologian is one who prays and one who prays is a theologian." Theology is knowledge that participates in God, that eats and drinks Christ in Communion, *Communion*, that seeks a connection with God. And because Orthodox theology is Orthodox knowing, as described above, books can have value but can never contain theology.

In the West, some Christians regard Christianity as a system of ideas. Hence one Catholic author writes, "It is fatal to let people suppose that Christianity is only a mode of feeling; it is vitally necessary to insist that it is first and foremost a rational explanation of the universe." If this is not universal among Western Christians, it nonetheless represents one of the threads that keeps popping up.

Eastern Orthodox would agree that Christianity is not primarily a mode of feeling; indeed, Orthodox do not believe that feelings are the measure of worship. But we part company with the Catholic author quoted, in trying to fix this by placing a system of ideas where some place emotion.

Orthodoxy is a *way*, just as many Eastern religions are a way. It is a path one walks. A worldview is something you believe and through which you see things; those elements are present in a way, but a way is something you do. It is like a habit, or even better a skill, which you start at clumsily and with time you not only become better at, but it becomes more natural. But it is more than a skill. It is even more encompassing than a worldview; it is how you approach life. Part of the West says we must each forge our own way; Orthodoxy invites people into the way forged by Christ, but it very much sees the importance of walking in a way.

The West tends to treat society as to a raw material, a despicable raw material, which will begin to have goodness if one puts goodness into it, transforming it according to one's enlightened vision.

This undergirds not only liberalism but most criticism of "common Western tendencies", and in particular most Christian attempts at counterculture. This attitude behind counterculture is not only that the Fall has impacted one's culture, but that there is nothing really good or authoritative about culture unless one puts it in.

Counterculture tends to be seen as essentially good.

In the East, as in the medieval and ancient West, the assumed relationship between a man and his culture is like the relationship between a man and his mother. It is a relationship which respects authority, femininity, and kinship.

This is not to say that one's culture cannot be wrong. What it is to say is that there is a world of difference between saying, "Mother, you are wrong," and "You are not my mother! You are nothing but a despicable raw material which it is my position to put something good in by transforming it according to my ideas." There can in fact be counterculture, but it is not counterculture according to the example of the Renaissance magus, the Enlightenment (or contemporary liberal) social engineer, or the postmodern deconstructionist. It is rather like the wild offshoot into Christ's body the Church, who regards his mother the Church, and patristic culture, as more authoritative than the culture he was born in.

Counterculture can be seen as a necessary evil.

What the Incarnation Means

In the West, doctrines have worked like elements in a philosophical system, while in the East, the focus is on what doctrines mean for us. There is a difference of focus, more than ideas contained, in the doctrine of the Trinity. The Western emphasis has been on philosophical clarity in describing the Father, Son, and Holy Spirit. The Eastern emphasis has been on what the persons of the Trinity mean for us and how we relate to them.

The Church didn't even spell out a philosophical analysis of the Trinity until almost three centuries had passed and a heresy contradicted what they had always known. The Church had always known that the Son and the Holy Spirit were just as divine as the Father, and it taught people to appropriately relate to the Father, Son, and Holy Spirit before it spelled out why people should relate that way.

The Incarnation, God becoming human, is recognized by all Christians who have their heads screwed on straight (and quite a few who don't). But in the East, believing in the Incarnation isn't just an idea that we agree with (although that is important). It is something that in practice determines the shape of a great many things in our spiritual walk. It is something that has great practical relevance. I would like to explain some of what the Incarnation means in the East, and that means explaining how the Incarnation gives shape to our spiritual walk.

There has been a saying rumbling down through the ages. The Son of God became a man that men might become the Sons of God (Protestant). The divine became man so that man might become divine (Catholic). God and the Son of God became man and the Son of Man that men might become gods and the sons of God. This teaching has mostly fallen away in Protestantism, even if Luther and Calvin believed it, and it is one puzzle piece among others in Catholicism. To the Orthodox it is foundational. The whole purpose of Christ becoming man, and our becoming

Christian, is to become like Christ. Furthermore, becoming like Christ does not simply mean becoming like Jesus the morally good and religious man without reference to Christ's divinity. We don't split Christ like that. If God wants to make us like Christ, he wants to make us like Christ who is fully God and fully human, and that means that we "share in the divine nature" (as spelled out in II Pet 1:4). It means that if we read Paul talking about the Son of God as meaning divinity, then when Paul talks about us as sons of God he is saying something in the same vein. There are caveats the Orthodox believe that help balance the picture--in particular, we can be made divine by grace, but only God can be divine by nature, ever. We cannot make others divine. God has his essence which is beyond knowing and his energies which reach out to us, but we can never reach beyond his manifest energies to see his essence. Catholics believe in a "beatific vision" that in Heaven we will see God as he truly is. Orthodox call that heresy. God can reach out to us and we can meet him when he reaches out, but it is radically, utterly, and absolutely impossible for us to ever know God as he truly is. Neither our being divine by grace nor our glorification in Heaven can ever overcome God's absolute transcendence. The Orthodox liturgy and prayers not only take account of sin; they spend more time bringing sin we need to repent of before God, than our being made like Christ. With all these caveats, the basic picture means that the Incarnation is not a one-time unnatural exception, something which runs against the grain of how God operates, or something totally unlike what can happen with us. The Incarnation is a peerless model that established the pattern of what it means to be Christian. Christ as the example of who a Christian should be is the only human who was fully divine, and even the only one to be fully human, but the Christian walk was meant to be, *and is*, a symbol that both represents and embodies what happened in the Incarnation. Christ is really incarnate in every member of the Church, and the Incarnation is not an anti-natural exception, but the pattern for being Christian. The purpose of being Christian is what Orthodox call "theosis," or "divinization," or "deification."

Part of understanding that Christ became human, and in fact became flesh, requires an understanding of how spirit and matter relate. DesCartes is one of the more Western philosophers. Part of his contribution was a lot of thinking about the famous problem of the "ghost in the machine." The problem of the "ghost in the machine" is the problem of how our minds can interact with our bodies, once you put mind and body in watertight compartments and assume that they shouldn't be able to interact. It's possible to be Western and disagree with DesCartes--but the main Western starting point is that mind and body are things one would expect to be separate.

In the East we don't have trouble with the "ghost in the machine" problem because we don't treat matter and spirit as things that are cut off from each other. We believe that matter and spirit are tightly bound together. It doesn't seem strange to us that our minds can move our bodies--it's a wonder, as all of God's works are wonders, but it's not something illogical.

This understanding means that the Incarnation doesn't just mean that Christ had a body; it means that Christ was connected to his body on the most intimate level. What the Incarnation means for us isn't just that Christ's body, and our bodies, are somehow part of the picture. It means that our bodies are an *inescapable* part of the picture, and they are very relevant to our spirits.

If you visit Orthodox worship, you may wonder why people stand, cross themselves, bow, kiss icons, and so on and so forth--in short, why their bodies are so active. The answer is that since our spirits and bodies are tied together in the whole person, worship includes the whole person. We don't just park our bodies while our spirits get on with worship. We might do that if we thought that our minds and bodies were separate, but we don't. We believe that Christ's incarnation is a matter of the Son of God, and the man's spirit, mind, soul, *and body* making one being, Christ, who was as united as possible. And that means that worship at Church and the broader spiritual walk both involve the whole person.

This integrated view of spirit and matter, and of the Incarnation, helps create the space for icons. I found icons strange at first, largely because as a Western Christian I had no place for icons that was appropriate. Believing that physical matter can have spiritual properties, that an icon can embody a real presence, all seems strange to someone shaped by nominalism and a rigid separation of spirit and matter. But I am learning to appreciate that to an Orthodox, to say that Christ had a body and to say that matter and spirit are tied together paves the way to recognizing that icons are a gift from God. They mean that matter is not cut off from spirit when it comes to our bodies, and they mean that matter is not cut off from spirit in places where we worship. Icons are another part of the incarnate faith of the Orthodox Church, and if you disagree with them, please understand that they are part of the understanding of how the Incarnation tells us practically how the Father wants us to worship him.

When I was a Protestant, the songs I heard in Church were about spiritual themes, and more specifically they are about themes in the Bible that seem spiritual and theological given a watertight idea of spirit. As contrasted to the Psalms, there was almost none of the imagery of the natural world. Orthodox liturgy, which contains a lot of teaching, sweeps across the both material and spiritual creation. One hymn praises Mary, the mother of our Lord, as "the volume [book] on which the Word [Christ] was inscribed," and "the ewe that bore the Lamb of God." The frequent physical and nature imagery that seamlessly praises God and rejoices in his whole creation is what being spiritual looks like when spirit is recognized as so deeply connected with the material dimension to our Lord's creation.

Like other Eastern religions, Orthodoxy has a supportive framework of formal and informal prayer, fasting from foods, ritual worship, hesychasm (stillness) and other aspects of spiritual discipline (which some Orthodox call "ascesis"). These are not "rules," but they do provide a concrete structure to help people. Partly because Orthodoxy assumes the relevance of matter to being spiritual, Orthodoxy doesn't just say "Go, be spiritual," without giving further direction as it doesn't just say "Park your bodies so your spirits can worship." The structure provided for spiritual discipline is shaped by the Incarnation, and not only because it addresses the whole person. The spiritual discipline is not very different from other Eastern religions, but the meaning of that spiritual discipline is very different. In Hinduism and Buddhism, asceticism is something you do for yourself, and other people often aren't part of the picture. When the Buddha decided to turn back and share his discovery with others, he was choosing a second best--according to Buddhism, the best thing would have been to enter complete release (salvation) instead of compromising his own benefit to share his discovery with others. Being good to other people, in Buddhism and in Hinduism tends to be like a boat you use to cross a river: once you have crossed the river, you don't need the boat any more.

What about Orthodoxy? One Orthodox saying is, "We are saved in community. We are condemned all by ourselves." Another Orthodox saying puts it even more strongly: "We can't be saved. The Church is saved, and we can be in it." Orthodox spiritual discipline is not something that makes ethics unnecessary. The whole point of spiritual discipline is ethical. If I pursue asceticism, the goal isn't for me to be saved all by myself; it is impossible for me to be saved all by myself, just like it's impossible for me to have a good friendship all by myself. The goal of asceticism is for the Orthodox to love God and his neighbor, and if someone fails to recognize this, this is a problem. Spiritual discipline is Incarnational because, as much as the Incarnation was an act of love for others, spiritual discipline is oriented to loving with Christ's own love.

In the West, people see salvation as accomplished through Christ's cross; in Orthodoxy, we believe that Christ's whole time on earth, including the cross, saves us. "Incarnation" means not only the moment when the Son of God became a man, but his baptism, ministry, cross, tomb, and resurrection. And thus the Incarnation I have discussed above is not simply the moment when the Son of God became a man, but Christ's whole coming that saves us.

Ella Enchanted

The movie *Ella Enchanted* has beautiful fantasy-themed computer graphics. Ella, the daughter of a nobleman, lives in a lovely Gothic-looking house in the middle of a suburban yard, goes down a lovely rustic-looking wooden escalator complete with a rustic-looking peasant turning a manual cogwheel, and is surrounded by stained glass windows and other medieval-looking trappings when she goes to her coed community college and gets into a debate about government policy and racial exploitation. One of the characters is an elf who wants to break out of the stereotype and be a lawyer instead of an entertainer (which is prohibited by law), and one of the nice things that happens at the happy ending is that the elf and a giantess fall in love with each other.

This movie is not just historically inaccurate; it is historically irrelevant, and it wears its historical irrelevancy with flamboyance. Everything you see has a medieval theme. The lovely Gothic-looking architecture, the richly colored medieval-looking clothing, and the swords and armor all tried to communicate the medieval. And it would be horribly unfair to treat the film as a botched version of historical accuracy, because it simply wasn't playing that game. However much things had been made to look "medieval," to someone who didn't understand the Middle Ages, it wasn't even *pretending* to faithfully represent that era. It was using the medieval as a projection screen as a whimsical place to address today's concerns. That was its real job.

That basic phenomenon affects a lot of how the West tries to understand the East, even when it *is* trying to faithfully represent it. In *Ella Enchanted* it is intentional, and the effect must be seen to be believed. (But then, that may be too high of a price to pay--as has been said about another movie.) I was appalled when I visited Victor Hugo's house, heard about Victor

Hugo's fashionable interest in the Orient, and saw an Oriental-themed wooden painting of Chinese acrobats using their bodies to make a V and an H for "Victor Hugo." China has produced acrobats, and Chinese acrobats are presumably capable of making those shapes with their bodies. But is this China, even allowing for cultural translation errors?

One major thread in most cultures outside the West is a tendency to exalt the whole of society and de-emphasize the individual person; indeed, people are seen without the Western concept of an "individual." Individualism is historically anomalous, and having acrobats shape their bodies to the greater glory of Victor Hugo would be about as out of place in Chinese culture as a large pro-censorship demonstration would be at an American university. Here and in other places, the "East" is not really the East, even an imperfectly understood East, but a projection screen for use by the West. *Ella Enchanted* was tongue-in-cheek and knew what was going on, where this was serious (and didn't know what was going on), but they were both using exotic places as a projection screen rather than something understood in itself.

New Age quotes the East, as well as "anything but the modern West," and it has its various attempts to create an alternative to traditional society. The East is over-represented in terms of spiritual practices and ideas, but I suggest that the same thing is going on here as *Ella Enchanted* or the supposedly Chinese acrobats celebrating the greater glory of Victor Hugo. In other words, we have a projection screen (in this case, non-Western) being used to project a thoroughly Western approach to life. The forces displayed are much an exaggeration of things that are accepted in Protestant Christianity.

What is the Western element that is found in New Age?

In the West, heresy is understood as condemned ideas. But the word "heresy" comes from a Greek word meaning "choice," and in the East heresy is making a private choice apart from the Orthodox Church. This can mean rejecting Church teaching, or splitting off from the Church, but the core of heresy is not the destructively false idea but the private choice. (This already has implications for the American definition of religion as a private choice.)

New Age is Gnostic, but there is something interesting in how it departs from ancient Gnosticism. Ancient Gnosticism was not a single, unified movement, but a broad collection of related but quite different movements with conflicting ideas. In this sense it was like New Age, and for that matter there is a certain deja vu between New Age and ancient Gnosticism. What's interesting is how New Age is unlike Gnosticism.

Gnostics had a lot of different ideas that conflicted not only with Orthodox Christianity but with each other. *And they argued.* Gnostics argued with other Gnostics and with Christians. Agreeing to disagree was as foreign to the Gnostics as it was to the Orthodox Christians. Saying "That's true for you, but this is true for me" or "That's your choice but this is my choice" would be as strange in classical Gnosticism as an escalator would have been in the Middle Ages.

New Age is a choice, and it is even more of a choice than in Gnosticism in its classical forms. Yes, the ideas are often Gnostic. Yes, New Age gives many of its members permission to indulge in magical, sexual, pride-related, and other sins, almost the same list as what ancient Gnosticism gave its members license for. But the essence of New Age is about a *choice*, the kind of choice that undergirds heresy. You choose (within certain broad parameters) what you will believe, what your spiritual practices will be, and so on and so forth, and the religion you practice is the sum of the private choices you make.

Where does this idea of religion as defined by private choice come from? One gets the impression from the New Age that it is the wisdom of the East to recognize that all religions say the same thing, and that a sort of Western style inquisition wouldn't happen. And that is true. *Kind of.*

In English, poetic license is a legitimate aspect of the language. And there isn't any central authority to approve instances of poetic license, nor can a poet be expelled from the

English Speaker's Guild for abusing the language. But if one simply tears up the English language, it loses its coherence as English. And so there is poetic license in English, but that doesn't mean that anything goes. And in Hinduism, for instance, there is no centralized authority and no systematic purge of heretics, but that doesn't mean that a Hindu (or Buddhist, etc.) approves of religion being approached as a salad bar. Leaders in many Eastern religions may say that all religions are equivalent, and Japanese are often both Buddist and Shinto, but most Eastern religious leaders would rather have you be coherently Christian, or Taoist, or Buddhist, or Hindu, or Jain, than simultaneously try to mix being Christian, *and* Taoist, *and* Buddhist, *and* Jain. That kind of incoherence is not very Eastern in spirit, nor is the idea of creating your own religion particularly Eastern.

What does Orthodoxy say? It matters whether or not you are Christian, and it matters whether or not you are Orthodox. But there is a saying that we can tell where the Church is, but not where it isn't. There is real truth in all religions, and if the Orthodox Church claims to be the fullness of Christ's Church, she would never claim that Christ's Church is limited to her walls. And her rules mean something different from in the West; instead of meaning "You must or must not do ________," they are resources that your spiritual father can use in addressing the specifics of your situation. In Orthodoxy your spiritual father helps decide what you are going to observe instead of you making the decision on your own, but the rules are more guidelines that your spiritual father can use in meeting the specifics of your situation, than rules in the Western sense. "Oikonomia" is an official recognition that your priest can work with you to figure out how Orthodoxy plays out in your situation.

Which brings me to the Reformation. Martin Luther did something original, but it was not the substance of his criticisms. Almost everything he had said was said earlier by someone else; there were things a lot like the Reformation floating around. Nor would Luther claim to have originated his criticisms much more than a baseball coach telling a boy to "Keep your eye on the ball" would claim to be the first one to give that advice. Luther didn't get his historic position solely by copying other people, but if you seek new criticisms from him, you're barking up the wrong tree.

Did Martin Luther contribute anything new? His criticisms had generally been circulating in the Catholic Church. An Orthodox might say that the Catholic Church had drifted from its Orthodox roots even further since 1054, when the Catholic Church broke off from the Orthodox Church. An Orthodox might interpret the general malaise in the Catholic Church as a malaise precisely because it had drifted from its Orthodox roots, and that the Orthodox Church agrees with the vast majority of Luther's criticisms (as for that matter the Catholic Church has--it acted on many of Luther's criticisms). Then what was new about Luther? Is Luther famous for an obscure reason?

Unless I am convinced by Scripture and plain reason--I do not accept the authority of Popes and councils, for they have contradicted each other--my conscience is captive to the Word of God. I cannot and will not recant anything, for to go against conscience is neither right nor safe.

After Luther said this, he split the Church. This is a rousing statement, and it is a rousing statement that contains the heart of heresy. A heretic is not so much someone who has a wrong idea, but someone who has a wrong idea *and is willing to split the Church over it*. Luther's distinctive and historic contribution was not levelling particular criticisms against the Catholic Church, but *choosing* to split the Church rather than go against his conscience, and his understanding of Scripture and plain reason. This choice is at the very heart of heresy.

Luther was a monumental figure, a great hero and a great villain rolled into one. His courage was monumental; so was his anti-semitism. And Luther was a prime example of a heretic. He was a heretic not so much by the points which he had wrong, which are relatively unimportant, but because he defined the Reformation with his precedent of splitting the Church.

So Luther worked to establish the re-established ancient Christian Church, and I am not particularly concerned here with the ways the re-established ancient Christian Church served as a projection screen for ideas that were in vogue at the time. (Somehow, when people re-establish ancient glory, their work ends up with a large dose of ideas that are in vogue with their creators. It happens again and again, and I think it has to do with how the ancient glory serves as a projection screen, much like New Age.) That tendency aside, Luther and the Catholic Church treated each other as heretics for a very good reason. It wasn't that they weren't ecumenical enough, or that they needed to be more tolerant, or that they needed to be told they were all Christians and Christianity is Christianity. The reason was something else. I can lament the blood that was shed, but there was a very healthy reason why people went that far against their opponents.

The Catholic Church, along with Luther, and for that matter along with the Orthodox, recognized that there is one Church, bound together in a full communion that cannot exist without agreement in doctrinal matters. Luther's reconstituted Church and the Catholic Church differed in doctrine and could not have this common basis. If you have two different groups which differ in doctrine, at least one of them is not the true Church. This is for the same reason that if one person says that an airplane is in Canada and another person says the same airplane is in Mexico, at least one of them has to be wrong. They could both be wrong; nothing rules that out. Luther and the Catholic Church might neither be the true Church. But if there are two conflicting organizations competing to be called the true Church, at least one of them has to be wrong, just as an airplane cannot simultaneously be in Canada and in Mexico. Luther and the Catholic Church both recognized this.

What one might have expected, if Luther were simply re-establishing what the Christian Church was in ancient times, was that there would be one and only reformer's Church. When Luther couldn't agree with other reformers, they split off from each other, each saying, "We're the true Church!" "No, we're the true Church!" It wasn't long until there were seventy or so different groups, and the claim, "We're the true Church" could no longer be taken seriously. In retrospect, Luther's saying "I do not accept the authority of Popes and councils, for they have contradicted each other," and then moving to Protestant churches was a move out of the frying pan and into the fire. Perhaps Luther could not have foreseen this unintended consequence, but the disagreements and divisions in Luther's wake made the disagreements of Popes and councils pale in comparison.

At that point, the reformers reconsidered what was going on, but they chose to consider the Church structure generated by the Reformation as valid. There was an unwritten rule: "Whatever you say about churches, it has to approve of what's happened with the Reformation splintering into many groups that could not be in communion with each other, no matter what Christians have believed about Church since the days of the Apostles themselves."

The solution they invented included the concept of a "denomination". The idea was that these different groups were not competitors for the title of "true Church;" instead, they were simply names for parts of the true Church. The true Church was not a unified organism complete with authority as it had been understood from the days of the apostles; it was something invisible and quite independent of formal structures. It's kind of like there had been a supercomputer club whose charter said that they would have one supercomputer, but they couldn't agree on which computer was the most appropriate supercomputer, so they violated the club charter by each buying his own computer, and to be able to say they had one computer like the charter said, hooked the computers up and said that the real club supercomputer was something invisible, a sort of virtual computer, that was emulated over the club network--and then said that this is what the original charter *really* called for. This is *not* because the reformers read the Bible and this was the best picture they could come up with of what the Church should be. It was much closer to an answer to the question of "How can we re-imagine Church so it won't look like the Bible condemns the church structures which the Reformation can't escape?"

Today we have:

- All denominations point to the same Christian truth.

- It doesn't matter which denomination you're part of, as long as you have faith.

- It doesn't matter much whether you stick to one denomination's prayers, doctrines, and so on and so forth, or for that matter whether you consider yourself a member of one denomination at all.

- We should pursue the goal of uniting all the different denominations.

But let me change barely more than one term:

- All religions point to the same truth.

- It doesn't matter which religion you're part of, as long as you have faith.

- It doesn't matter much whether you stick to one religion's prayers, doctrines, and so on and so forth, or for that matter whether you consider yourself a member of one religion at all.

- We should pursue the goal of uniting all the different religions.

Sound familiar? It should. It's New Age. It's the foundation to the New Age movement that all the exotic Asian decor rests on, and it is more Western than most of the West. Or at least there's an uncanny resemblance between Protestantism and something most Protestants wouldn't want to be associated with. (Or at least evangelicals wouldn't want to be associated with New Age. With mainline, er, oldline, er, sideline, er, flatline Protestantism, the line between "Protestant" and "New Age" is often crystal clear, but at other times can be maddeningly difficult to tell the difference.) Beyond all New Age's Eastern trappings, the heart of the New Age is a non-Christian twist on a very Western way of thinking about religious community. That way of thinking is the Protestant understanding of Church.

Why am I making such a disturbing and perhaps offensive connection? Do I believe Protestantism is as bad as New Age? Absolutely not; I think there's a world of difference. The answer has to do with something else, something about Orthodoxy that seems strange to many Protestants. What is this something else?

Jesus, in the great prayer recorded before his execution, prayed fervently that all his disciples may be one, and Paul made incendiary remarks whenever he discussed people having different denominations. So it is important for all Christians to be united, and that goes for Orthodox. So why do Orthodox refuse to attend non-Orthodox worship and especially to take non-Orthodox communion? Why do we exclude non-Orthodox from our own communion cups? So why don't Orthodox recognize that we are just one more denomination, even if we are a very old denomination? Why are there so few Orthodox at ecumenical gatherings?

Something has to give, and Protestants often try to figure out whether the observations about Orthodoxy are what gives, or whether Orthodox really being Christians gives. Which one gives? *Neither.* Neither the practices that seem so strange to Protestant ecumenism, nor the imperative to Christian unity, give. What give are the Protestant assumptions about what makes Church, that determines what Protestants see as real ecumenism.

I've written a long and subtle discussion about *Ella Enchanted*, New Age, and other things because I wanted to get to this point. New Age may do all sorts of things to get an impression of being Eastern, and it may be chock full of exotic decor. But underneath that decor is something very Western. It is a modified form of Protestant teachings about Church. The similarity between:

- All denominations point to the same Christian truth.

- It doesn't matter which denomination you're part of, as long as you have faith.

- It doesn't matter much whether you stick to one denomination's prayers, doctrines, and so on and so forth, or for that matter whether you consider yourself a member of one denomination at all.

- We should pursue the goal of uniting all the different denominations.

and:

- All religions point to the same truth.

- It doesn't matter which religion you're part of, as long as you have faith.

- It doesn't matter much whether you stick to one religion's prayers, doctrines, and so on and so forth, or for that matter whether you consider yourself a member of one religion at all.

- We should pursue the goal of uniting all the different religions.

is a disturbing similarity. And most evangelicals wouldn't touch the second list of statements with a ten foot pole. Yet it is connected to the first statement. The first set of statements isn't what the Bible says. It isn't what Christians have believed from ancient times. Its job was to give a rubber stamp to the sort of churches the Reformation created, and serve as a substitute for what the Orthodox believe about Church. And, with modifications, that way of thinking about Church has been perfectly happy to abandon Christianity and help give us the New Age movement.

My purpose isn't to get you to reject Protestant assumptions about church. But it is my purpose to help you see that they are assumptions, and that Orthodox have worshipped God for two millenia with a quite different set of assumptions. If you can see your own objection to New Age treating all religions as interchangeable, you may be able to see the Orthodox objection to treating all denominations as interchangeable, even if it's on a smaller scale. And to show why Orthodox do not simply see the Protestant style of ecumenism as necessary to a full and robust obedience to the commandment to Christian unity.

The Focus

In Chinese translations of the Bible, the main rendering of Logos (Word in the prologue to John) is Tao, a concept in both Taoism and Confucianism which is important to Chinese thought and includes the Eastern concept of a Way. In Chinese translations, the prologue opens, "In the beginning was the Tao, and the Tao was with God, and the Tao was God." Is this appropriate?

"Tao" translates "Logos" better than any word that is common in English, and the real question is not whether it is appropriate for the Chinese to render "Logos" with their "Tao," but whether it is appropriate for us to render "Logos" with our much less potent "Word," which is kind of like undertranslating "breathtaking" as "not bad."

Is it OK to mix Christianity and Taoism? There are important incompatibilities but my reading the classic Taoist *Tao Te Ching* put me in a much better position to understand Christ the Logos and the Christian Way than I would have otherwise had. God has not left himself without a witness, and Taoism resonates with Orthodoxy.

In fact, there are quite a lot of things that resonate with Orthodoxy; it would be difficult to think of two religions, or philosophies, or movements, that have absolutely no contact. It may be easy to forget this in the West; one of the Western mind's special strength is to analyze things by looking into their differences. This is a powerful ability. But it is not the only basic insight. Essentially any two grapplings with human and spiritual realities (religions/philosophies/movements) will have points of contact. It isn't just Taoism that resonates with Orthodoxy. Hinduism is deep and has a deep resonance with Orthodoxy. The fact that I have not said more about Hinduism is only because I don't know it very well, but I know that it is deep. Catholicism resonates with Orthodoxy even more than Western Christianity as a whole. Platonism resonates with Orthodoxy, and the Church Fathers learned from their day's Platonism, however much they tried to avoid uncritically accepting Platonism. For that matter, Gnosticism resonates with Orthodoxy. But isn't Gnosticism a heresy? Yes, and it couldn't have a heresy's sting unless it resonated with Orthodoxy. Part of a heresy's *job description* is to be confusingly similar to Orthodoxy. Postmodernism resonates with Orthodoxy. I wouldn't be surprised if some scholar has said, "Orthodoxy is postmodernism done right."

It should not come as a surprise that feminism resonates with Orthodoxy, evangelicalism, and the Bible. Jesus broke social rules in every recorded encounter with women in the Gospels. And "In Christ there is no Jew nor Greek, slave nor free, male nor female" is profound, and cannot be separated from the rest of the Gospel message. Looking at a historical context and a cultural context where feminism is floating around, where some form of feminism is the air people breathe--in other words, not the Early Church's context, but *our own* historical and cultural context (yes, we have one too!), it should come as no surprise that people see the Gospel as moving towards what we now call feminism, a moderate feminism of course, and so people work to develop a Biblical egalitarianism that will coax out the woman-friendly vision the Gospel is reaching towards, and correct certain abuses and misunderstandings of the Bible in its cultural context.

This should not come as a surprise. What I had originally thought to write is as follows: It is entirely understandable to try to adjust Christianity with a moderate feminism and try to help Christianity move in the direction it seems to have been moving towards, from the very beginning, but even if it is understandable it is not entirely correct. It is not entirely incorrect but it is not entirely correct either.

Christ's robe is a seamless robe that may not be torn. So is the Gospel. The same God inspired "In Christ there is neither Jew nor Greek, slave nor free, male nor female," and equally inspired, "Wives, submit to your husbands... Husbands, love your wives even as Christ loved the Church and gave himself up for her." *The same God who inspired one inspired the other,* and if your interpretation doesn't have room for both, it is your interpretation that needs to be adjusted, not God's revelation.

But what about cultural context? That question comes up a lot. And let me share some of what I found in my studies. I set out to do a thesis on how to tell when a book which treats a Bible passage's cultural context is misusing the context to neutralize a pesky passage that says something the scholar doesn't like. The first time I heard that someone had made an in-depth study of a pesky passage's cultural context and it turned out that the pesky passage meant something very different from what it appeared to mean, I believed it. I fell hook, line, and sinker. But after a while, I began to grow suspicious. It seemed that "taking the cultural context into consideration" turned out to mean "the pesky passage isn't a problem" again and again. And I began to study. That seemed to happen with every egalitarian treatment of one particular important passage--not only that I could find, but that my thesis advisor could find, and my advisor was a respected egalitarian scholar who spoke at a Christians for Biblical Equality conference! There were a lot of things I found about using cultural context, and my advisor liked my thesis. But in the end, there is a simple answer to, "How can you tell, if a book studies a pesky passage's cultural context in depth and concludes that the passage doesn't mean anything for us that would interfere with what the scholar believes, if the book is misusing cultural context to neutralize the passage?" The answer is, "There will be ink on its pages."

"In Christ there is no male nor female" is true, and it is for very good reason that that resonates with feminists. What a Biblical Egalitarian or feminist may not realize is that there is also a truth which feminism does not especially sensitize people to. "God created man in his image" is tightly connected with "Male and female he created them." There is unity in Christ, and we are called to transcend ourselves, including being male and female. But when God invites us to transcend our creaturely state, that doesn't annihilate our creaturely state; it fulfills us--just as God's promise that our bodies which are sown in decay and weakness will be raised in power and glory. Christ's promise of a transformed resurrection body does not take away our bodies; it means that our bodies will be glorified with a depth we cannot imagine. Christ's establishment of a Church that transcends male and female does not mean that being male and female is now unimportant, but that God uses them in his Kingdom that is being built here on earth. Men and women are meant to be different, in a way that you're going to miss if you're trying to see who is greater than who else. Paul writes, "There are Heavenly bodies and there are earthly bodies; but the glory of the Heavenly is one, and the glory of the earthly is another. There is one glory of the sun, and another glory of the moon, and and another glory of the stars, and star differs from star in glory" (I Cor 15:40-41). If star differs from star in glory, so do women differ from men in glory. Men and women are different as colors are different, or as a blazing fire is different from a deep and shimmering pool. This is truth, and if you take the feminist truth alone and not the other side of the truth, you flatten out something that is best not to flatten out--and it makes a bigger difference than many people realize.

That's what I would have written earlier. What I would have focused on now is different. It seems that when people return to past glory, or *try* to return to past glory, the past resonates with what's in vogue, and we don't pick up on things people knew then that we aren't sensitive to now, or even worse we pick up on them but neutralize them. ("Man will occasionally stumble over the truth, but most of the time he will pick himself up and continue on.") We unwittingly make the past a projection screen for what is sensible to us--which often means what's in vogue. The Renaissance called for a return to past glory and ended up being an unprecedented break from the past. The same thing happened with the neo-classicist Enlightenment. And something like this happened with the Reformation. When you sever yourself from tradition to get to the past, you're cutting open a goose to get all the golden eggs.

Part of being Protestant, whether it is evangelical, or the more liberal *Prayers of the Cosmos: Meditations on the Aramaic Words of Christ* (note the effort to reach further back than even the Greek New Testament), or deconstruction to get to what a text really meant (so that the text agrees with deconstructionist revisions to morality)--part of all of this is the idea that you dig past the tradition's obstacles and barnacles to unearth the Bible's meaning, perhaps a meaning that is hidden from the common multitude who blindly accept tradition. The idea that tradition is a connection to the past seems to be obscured, and sometimes the result seems to be digging a hole with no bottom. There's no limit to how much tradition you can dig past in an attempt to reach the unvarnished text. And this phenomenon is foundational to Protestantism. There are things that distinguish evangelicals from liberal Protestants, but not the effort to liberate the text's original meaning. In that sense Biblical egalitarianism is a member in good standing of Protestant positions--not the only one, but one member in good standing. And if past glory has functioned as an ambiguous projection screen, this may mean that Biblical egalitarianism has problems. But it doesn't doesn't mean that Biblical egalitarianism is a different sort of thing from Protestantism. It may be an example of how a Protestant movement can misunderstand the Gospel.

Attempts to recover past glory **can** be for the better. One group of evangelicals, originally in a parachurch organization, came to realize that "parachurch" wasn't part of how Early Christians operated. There was no parachurch, only Church. So, assuming that the ancient Church disappeared, they agreed to research the ancient Church and each century's developments and follow them if they were appropriate, and founded the Evangelical Orthodox Church. They went some distance into this process before they ran into a Russian Orthodox priest, and they (the real Church) were examining the outsider, or so they thought... and they found that Orthodoxy preserved the ancient teaching about the Lord's body and blood, and about Church structure, and... things were suddenly upside-down. The ancient Christian Church had not dried up. It was alive and well; they had simply overlooked it when they tried to re-create the ancient Church. It was *they* who were the outsiders. And they realized they needed to be received into the Orthodox Church.

My parish was Evangelical Orthodox before it became part of the Orthodox communion, which I think is special. So Evangelical Orthodoxy turned out all right. Why then would Biblical egalitarianism have gone wrong? That's not the puzzle. The puzzle is Evangelical Orthodoxy. Evangelical Orthodoxy is a surprise much like getting an envelope that says "Extremely important--open immediately!" and finding that it has something extremely important that needs to be opened immediately. Usually "Extremely important--open immediately" is a red flag which suggests that the contents of the envelope are something other than what you're being led to believe.

But my focus is not to say who's wrong and who's right in the Protestant theme of recovering the glory of the Early Church. It's not even to suggest that tradition is a mediator that connects us with past glory, a living link, instead of an obstacle which chiefly gets in our way. My focus is to talk about something that looms this large in Orthodoxy.

Orthodoxy is not understood best as the content of a private choice, any more than learning physics is privately choosing ideas about how the world works. In one sense it's hard to out-argue someone who says that, but that isn't a very Orthodox way of thinking. It could be called using Orthodoxy as if it were a private heresy. (Once I wanted to be Orthodox out of that kind of desire, and God said, "No.") It's also deceptive to say that a convert Orthodox should select Orthodoxy as a sort of winner in the contest of "Will the real ancient Church please stand up?" which he's judging. It's truer to say that that happens for many former evangelicals (including Your Truly) than I would like to admit, but Orthodoxy points to something deeper.

Repentance (which some Orthodox call "metanoia") looms almost as large in Eastern Orthodoxy as recovering the past glory of the ancient Church looms large in Western Protestantism. For that matter, it might loom larger. And I'd like to comment on what repentance is. This may or may not be very different from Western understandings of repentance--I learned much about repentance as an evangelical--but it would be worth clarifying.

Repentance is not just a matter of admitting that you're wrong and deciding you'll try to do better the next time. That's what repentance would be if God's grace were irrelevant. But God's grace is key to repentance. Grace isn't just something that God gives you after you repent. Repentance itself is a work of grace.

If repentance isn't simply admitting your error and deciding you want to do better, then what else is repentance? In this case, Orthodoxy becomes clearer if it is compared and contrasted with other Middle Eastern or Eastern religions.

"Islam" means "submission," and "Muslim" means "one who submits to God." Submission is not one feature of Islam among others; it is foundational to the landscape, and one of the deepest criticisms of Islam is that the Islamic way of understanding submission, and the Islamic picture of God, effectively deny the reality of man. How does Islam deny the reality of man? God alone contributes to the world's story. The only real place for us is virtual puppets--not people who help decide what goes into the story. But Islam's central emphasis on submission is itself something that's not too far from Orthodoxy.

In Hinduism and Buddhism, one of the defining goals is to transcend the self and become selfless, and both Hinduism and Buddhism believe this requires the annihilation of the self. In some of Hinduism, salvation means that the self dissolves in God like a drop of water returning to the ocean. In therevada Buddhism, to be saved is to be annihilated altogether.

Orthodoxy, by contrast, is deeply connected with the Gospel words, "Whoever finds his life will lose it, and whoever loses his life for my sake and for the sake of the Gospel will find it." (Mark 8:35) One of Orthodoxy's founding goals is to become selfless and transcending oneself--offering oneself totally and wholly to God, saying, "Strike me and heal me; cast me down and raise me up, whatever you will to do." This is how Orthodoxy believes in transcending one's being male and female: something that is totally offered up to God and which God, instead of annihilating, breathes his spirit into. This is the difference between Orthodoxy on the one hand, and on the other hand Hinduism, Buddhism, Islam, and even moderate feminism. Unlike Islam's picture, whoever totally submits to God, or strives for submission, hears God's voice boom forth, "Come! I want you to contribute to the story of my Creation! I want you to work alongside me!" The goal of Orthodoxy, or one of its defining goals, is to help each person to be fully who God created him or her to be.

What does this have to do with repentance?

Repentance means losing yourself. It means unconditional surrender. Losing yourself for Christ's sake and for the sake of the Gospel is transformed to mean finding yourself. Repentance is unconditional surrender, and it is one of the most terrifying things a person can experience. It's much more than letting go of a sin and saying, "I'm sorry." It's letting go of yourself. It's obeying God when he says, "I want you to write me a blank check." Perhaps afterwards you may be surprised how little money God actually wrote the check for--I am astonished at times--but God insists on us writing a blank check. God tells us to place our treasures, our sins, our very selves at his feet, for him to do whatever he wants, and that is absolutely terrifying. *Repentance isn't letting go of sin. It is unconditional surrender to God.* And it's the only way to transcend the self and become a selfless and transformed "me."

One pastor used the image (he held up his keys when he said this) that we've given God absolutely all of our keys--all but one, that is. And God is saying, "Give me that one," and we're giving God *anything* but that. God demands unconditional surrender, and he calls for unconditional surrender so that we can be free, truly free. In my own life I've offered God all sorts of consolation prizes, all sorts of substitutes for what he was asking me, and when I did let go, I realized that I was holding onto a piece of Hell. Before it is terrifying to let go, and then after I let go of my sin, I am horrified to realize that I was holding on to a smouldering piece of Hell itself. A recovering alcoholic will tell you that rejecting tightly held denial is something that an alcoholic will do absolutely anything to avoid--and that rejecting to denial is the only way to be freed from bondage to alcohol. That is very much what Orthodoxy announces about repenting from our sin.

Hell is not something external that will be added to sin starting in the afterlife. Every sin is itself the beginning of Hell. Orthodox theology says that the gates of Hell are bolted, barred, and sealed *from the inside*. It's not so much that God casts people into Hell as that Hell is a place people refuse to leave: Hell's motto may be, "It is better to reign in Hell than serve into Heaven." Hell is where God leaves people when they refuse to unbolt its gates and open themselves to the Father's love. I've experienced the beginning of Hell, and the beginning of Heaven, and you've experienced them both. Every sin is a seed that will grow into Hell unless we let God uproot it, and that means letting him dig however deep he wills.

Repentance needs to be not only admitting to a sin, but an unconditional surrender that leans on God's grace because apart from God it is beyond us. Repentance needs to be unconditional surrender because only when we give God our last key will we be released from holding on to that one piece of Hell we are trying to avoid giving to God. Repentance is a work of grace, both in God taking the piece of Hell we were clinging to, and in God's power helping us give us the strength to let go of that one piece of Hell.

That much is true, but this article is incomplete even as a tour guide. I'm not even sure it's an accurate picture of Orthodoxy. There's a joyful dance, a dance of grace and ever-expanding freedom, and this article is a still, flat picture of that dance. Everything I describe is meant as Orthodox, but I have flattened out its living energy (which is why this is so philosophical), without doing it justice. The solution is not a better and more complete picture of the dance that will still be flat and still. The solution is for you to see the dance live, whether or not these observations are what God wants you to see. God may want to show you things I've never hinted at, or use something I've written to help you connect with Orthodox worship, or for that matter use this article as a key to open the treasurehouses of Orthodoxy. But that is God's choice. And he can also connect you with the here and now as many Orthodox emphasize, or make everyday life more and more a home for contemplation, or pick out other treasures that you need. We don't know our true needs-- God does, and he cares for them.

For Further Reading...

If you've read this far and want to know how you can read more, I have not succeeded very well at communicating. I'm not saying there aren't any good books out there. There are scores and scores, and I've even read some of them. I love to read. But please don't try to read five more books on Orthodoxy so you'll understand it better. *Please* don't.

Go visit a parish. Participate, and come to experience firsthand, for real, what this book is at best a tour guide to. Even if this tour guide helps you see things you might not pick up on your own, it's only the tour guide. The reality is the life that Orthodox live, and if you come to a service wanting to take something in, I will be surprised if nothing happens. Joining Orthodox worship (even just sitting or standing) and trying to take everything in, is like falling into a lifegiving river, being surrounded by its mighty currents, and coming to contact with a little bit of it. Don't worry if you don't understand everything that's going on. I serve at the altar as an adult acolyte, and I *certainly* don't understand all that's going on. But I don't need to. There's a saying that a mouse can only drink its fill from a river, and it's simply beside the point that we can't drink all the water in the river. We don't need to. What we can do is take away what we are ready for and drink our fill.

And if you still feel a bit intimidated, like most of this is too subtle to understand--don't worry. You don't need to understand it the Western way, by figuring out all the concepts in an article. The Eastern way is to go to an Orthodox Church, and let God teach you over time. If you do that, it doesn't matter how much or how little this article seemed easy to think about.

An Orthodox Looks at a Calvinist Looking at Orthodoxy

Jack Kinneer, an Orthodox Presbyterian minister and a D.Min. graduate of an Eastern Orthodox seminary, wrote a series of dense responses to his time at that seminary. The responses are generally concise, clear, and make the kind of observations that I like to make. My suspicion is that if Dr. Kineer is looking at things this way, there are a lot of other people who are looking at things the same way--but may not be able to put their finger on it. And he may have given voice to some things that Orthodox may wish to respond to.

Orthodoxy is difficult to understand, and I wrote a list of responses to some (not all) of the points he raises. I asked New Horizons, which printed his article, and they offered gracious permission to post with attribution, which is much appreciated. I believe that Dr. Kinneer's words open a good conversation, and I am trying to worthily follow up on his lead.

A Calvinist Looks at Orthodoxy
Jack D. Kinneer

During my studies at St. Vladimir's Orthodox Theological Seminary, I was often asked by students, "Are you Orthodox?" It always felt awkward to be asked such a question. I thought of myself as doctrinally orthodox. I was a minister in the Orthodox Presbyterian Church. So I thought I could claim the word *orthodox.*

But I did not belong to the communion of churches often called Eastern Orthodox, but more properly called simply Orthodox. I was not Greek Orthodox, Russian Orthodox, or Antiochian Orthodox. As far as the Orthodox at St. Vladimir's were concerned, I was not Orthodox, regardless of my agreement with them on various doctrines.

My studies at St. Vladimir's allowed me to become acquainted with Orthodoxy and to become friends with a number of Orthodox professors, priests, and seminarians. My diploma was even signed by Metropolitan Theodosius, the head of the Orthodox Church in America. From the Metropolitan to the seminarians, I was received kindly and treated with respect and friendliness.

I am not the only Calvinist to have become acquainted with Orthodoxy in recent years. Sadly, a number have not only made the acquaintance, but also left the Reformed faith for Orthodoxy. What is Orthodoxy and what is its appeal to some in the Reformed churches?

The Appeal of Orthodoxy

Since the days of the apostles, there have been Christian communities in such ancient cities as Alexandria in Egypt, Antioch in Syria, and Corinth in Greece. In such places, the Christian church grew, endured the tribulation of Roman persecution, and ultimately prevailed when the Roman Empire was officially converted to Christianity. But, unlike Christians in the western half of the Roman Empire, the eastern Christians did not submit to the claims of the bishop of Rome to be the earthly head of the entire church. And why should they have done so? The centers of Orthodox Christianity were as old as, or even older than, the church in Rome. All the great ecumenical councils took place in the East and were attended overwhelmingly by Christian leaders from the East, with only a smattering of representatives from the West. Indeed, most of the great theologians and writers of the ancient church (commonly called the Church Fathers) were Greek-speaking Christians in the East.

The Orthodox churches have descended in an unbroken succession of generations from these ancient roots. As the Orthodox see it, the Western church followed the bishop of Rome into schism (in part by adding a phrase to the Nicene Creed). So, from their perspective, we Protestants are the product of a schism off a schism. The Orthodox believe that they have continued unbroken the churches founded by the apostles. They allow that we Reformed may be Christians, but our churches are not part of the true church, our ordinations are not valid, and our sacraments are no sacraments at all.

The apparently apostolic roots of Orthodoxy provide much of its appeal for some evangelical Protestants. Furthermore, it is not burdened with such later Roman Catholic developments as the Papacy, purgatory, indulgences, the immaculate conception of Mary, and her assumption into heaven. Orthodoxy is ancient; it is unified in a way that Protestantism is not; it lacks most of the medieval doctrines and practices that gave rise to the Reformation. This gives it for many a fascinating appeal.

Part of that appeal is the rich liturgical heritage of Orthodoxy, with its elaborate liturgies, its glorious garbing of the clergy, and its gestures, symbols, and icons. If it is true that the distinctive mark of Reformed worship is simplicity, then even more so is glory the distinctive mark of Orthodox worship. Another appealing aspect of Orthodox worship is its otherness. It is mysterious, sensual, and, as the Orthodox see it, heavenly. Orthodox worship at its best makes you feel like you have been transported into one of the worship scenes in the book of Revelation. Of course, if the priest chants off-key or the choir sings poorly, it is not quite so wonderful.

There are many other things that could be mentioned, but I've mentioned the things that have particularly struck me. These are also the things that converts from Protestantism say attracted them.

The Shortcomings of Orthodoxy

So then, is this Orthodox Presbyterian about to drop the "Presbyterian" and become simply Orthodox? No! In my estimation, the shortcomings of Orthodoxy outweigh its many fascinations. A comparison of the Reformed faith with the Orthodox faith would be a massive undertaking, made all the more difficult because Orthodoxy has no doctrinal statement comparable to the Westminster Confession of Faith. Orthodoxy is the consensus of faith arising from the ancient Fathers and the ecumenical councils. This includes the forty-nine volumes of the Ante- and Post-Nicene Fathers, plus the writings of the hermits and monastics known collectively as the Desert Fathers! It would take an entire issue of *New Horizons* just to outline the topics to be covered in a comparison of Orthodoxy and Reformed Christianity. So the following comments are selective rather than systematic.

First, in my experience, the Orthodox do not understand justification by faith. Some reject it. Others tolerate it, but no one I met or read seemed to really understand it. Just as Protestants can make justification the whole (rather than the beginning) of the gospel, so the Orthodox tend to make sanctification (which they call "theosis" or deification) the whole gospel. In my estimation, this is a serious defect. It weakens the Orthodox understanding of the nature of saving faith.

Orthodoxy also has a real problem with nominal

members. Many Orthodox Christians have a very inadequate understanding of the gospel as Orthodoxy understands it. Their religion is often so intertwined with their ethnicity that being Russian or Greek becomes almost synonymous with being Orthodox. This is, by the way, a critique I heard from the lips of Orthodox leaders themselves. This is not nearly as serious a problem in Reformed churches because our preaching continually stresses the necessity for a personal, intimate trusting, receiving, and resting upon Jesus Christ alone for salvation. Such an emphasis is blurred among the Orthodox.

Second, the Orthodox have a very inadequate understanding of sovereign grace. It is not fair to say that they are Pelagians. (Pelagius was a Western Christian who denied original sin and taught that man's will is free to choose good.) But they are definitely not Augustinians (Calvinists) on sin and grace. In a conversation with professors and doctoral students about the nature of salvation, I quoted Ezekiel 36:26-27 as showing that there is a grace of God that precedes faith and enables that human response. One professor said in response, "I never thought of that verse in that way before." The Orthodox have not thought a lot about sin, regeneration, election, and so forth. Their view of original sin (a term which they avoid) falls far short of the teaching of Paul. Correspondingly, their understanding of Christ's atonement and God's calling is weak as well. Their views could best be described as undeveloped. If you want to see this for yourself, read Chrysostom on John 6:44-45, and then read Calvin on the same passage.

Third, the Orthodox are passionately committed to the use of icons (flat images of Christ, Mary, or a saint) in worship. Indeed, the annual Feast of Orthodoxy celebrates the restoration of icons to the churches at the end of the Iconoclast controversy (in a.d. 843). For the Orthodox, the making and venerating of icons is the mark of Orthodoxy--

showing that one really believes that God the Son, who is consubstantial with the Father, became also truly human. Since I did not venerate icons, I was repeatedly asked whether or not I really believed in the Incarnation. The Orthodox are deeply offended at the suggestion that their veneration of icons is a violation of the second commandment. But after listening patiently to their justifications, I am convinced that whatever their intentions may be, their practice is not biblical. However, our dialogue on the subject sent me back to the Bible to study the issue in a way that I had not done before. The critique I would offer now is considerably different than the traditional Reformed critique of the practice.

Finally, many of the Orthodox tend to have a lower view of the Bible than the ancient Fathers had. At least at St. Vladimir's, Orthodox scholars have been significantly influenced by higher-critical views of Scripture, especially as such views have developed in contemporary Roman Catholic scholarship. This is, however, a point of controversy among the Orthodox, just as it is among Catholics and Protestants. Orthodoxy also has its divisions between liberals and conservatives. But even those who are untainted by higher-critical views rarely accord to Scripture the authority that it claims for itself or which was accorded to it by the Fathers. The voice of Scripture is largely limited to the interpretations of Scripture found in the Fathers.

There is much else to be said. Orthodoxy is passionately committed to monasticism. Its liturgy includes prayers to Mary. And the Divine Liturgy, for all its antiquity, is the product of a long historical process. If you want to follow the "liturgy" that is unquestionably apostolic, then partake of the Lord's Supper, pray the Lord's Prayer, sing "psalms, hymns, and spiritual songs," and say "amen," "hallelujah," and "maranatha." Almost everything else in any liturgy is a later adaptation and development.

A Concluding Assessment

But these criticisms do not mean that we have nothing to learn from Orthodoxy. Just as the Orthodox have not thought a lot about matters that have consumed us (such as justification, the nature of Scripture, sovereign grace, and Christ's work on the cross), so we have not thought a lot about what have been their consuming passions: the Incarnation, the meaning of worship, the soul's perfection in the communicable attributes of God (which they call the energies of God), and the disciplines by which we grow in grace. Let us have the maturity to keep the faith as we know it, and to learn from others where we need to learn.

Orthodoxy in many ways fascinates me, but it does not claim my heart nor stir my soul as does the Reformed faith. My firsthand exposure to Orthodoxy has left me all the more convinced that on the essential matters of human sin, divine forgiveness, and Christ's atoning sacrifice, the Reformed faith is the biblical faith. I would love to see my Orthodox friends embrace a more biblical understanding of these matters. And I am grieved when Reformed friends sacrifice this greater good for the considerable but lesser goods of Orthodox liturgy and piety.

Dr. Kinneer is the director of Echo Hill Christian Study Center in Indian Head, Pa.

Reprinted from New Horizons of the Orthodox Presbyterian Church, as posted at http://www.opc.org/new_horizons/calvinist_on_orthodoxy.html. Used with permission.

I wrote the following reply:

Dear Dr. Kinneer;

First, on an Orthodox mailing list, I saw a copy of your "A Calvinist Looks at Orthodoxy." I would like to write a somewhat measured response that you might find of interest; please quote me if you like, preferably with attribution and a link to my website (http://JonathansCorner.com). I am a convert Orthodox and a graduate of Calvin College, for which I have fond memories, although I was never a Calvinist, merely a non-Calvinist Evangelical welcomed in the warm embrace of the community. I am presently a Ph.D. student in theology at Fordham and went to church for some time at St. Vladimir's Seminary and have friends there. I hope that you may find something of interest in my comments here.

Second, you talk about discussion of being Eastern Orthodox versus being orthodox. I would take this as a linguistically confusing matter of the English language, where even in spoken English the context clarifies whether (o)rthodox or (O)rthodox is the meaning intended by the speaker.

Third, I will be focusing mostly on matters I where I would at least suggest some further nuance, but your summary headed "The Appeal of Orthodoxy," among other things in the article, is a good sort of thing and the sort of thing I might find convenient to quote.

Fourth, the Orthodox consensus of faith is not a much longer and less manageable collection of texts than the Ante-Nicene Fathers and Nicene and Post-Nicene Fathers, combined with the even more massive Patrologia Graecae, and other patristic sources. I have said elsewhere that Western and particularly Protestant and Evangelical culture are at their core written cultures, and Orthodoxy is at its core an oral culture that makes use of writing--I could suggest that it was precisely the Reformation that is at the root of what we now know as literate culture. This means that Orthodoxy does not have, as its closest equivalent to the Westminster Confession, a backbreaking load of books that even patristics scholars can't read cover to cover; it means that *the closest Orthodox equivalent to Westminster Confession is not anything printed but something alive in the life* *and culture of the community.* (At very least this is true if you exclude the Nicene Creed, which is often considered "what Orthodox are supposed to believe.")

Fifth, regarding the words, "First, in my experience, the Orthodox do not understand justification by faith:" are you contending that former Evangelicals, who had an Evangelical understanding of justification by faith, were probably fairly devout Evangelicals, and are well-represented at St. Vladimir's Seminary, do not understand justification by faith?

There seems to be something going on here that is a mirror image of what you say below about icons: there, you complain about people assuming that if you don't hold the Orthodox position on icons, you don't understand the Christian doctrine of the incarnation; here, you seem in a mirror image to assume that if people don't have a Reformation-compatible understanding of justification by faith, you don't understand the Biblical teaching.

I wrote, for a novella I'm working on, *The Sign of the Grail*, a passage where the main character, an Evangelical, goes to an Orthodox liturgy, hears amidst the mysterious-sounding phrases a reading including "The just shall walk by faith," before the homily:

In the Name of the Father, and of the Son, and of the Holy Ghost. Amen.

One of the surprises in the Divine Comedy--to a few people at least--is that the Pope is in Hell. Or at least it's a surprise to people who know Dante was a devoted Catholic but don't recognize how good Patriarch John Paul and Patriarch Benedict have been; there have been some moments Catholics aren't proud of, and while Luther doesn't speak for Catholics today, he did put his finger on a lot of things that bothered people then. Now I remember an exasperated Catholic friend asking, "Don't some Protestants know anything else about the Catholic Church *besides* the problems we had in the sixteenth century?" And when Luther made a centerpiece out of what the Bible said about

"The righteous shall walk by faith," which was in the Bible's readings today, he changed it, chiefly by using it as a battle axe to attack his opponents and even things he didn't like in Scripture.

It's a little hard to see how Luther changed Paul, since in Paul the words are also a battle axe against legalistic opponents. Or at least it's hard to see directly. Paul, too, is quoting, and I'd like to say exactly what Paul is quoting.

In one of the minor prophets, Habakkuk, the prophet calls out to the Lord and decries the wickedness of those who should be worshiping the Lord. The Lord's response is to say that he's sending in the Babylonians to conquer, and if you want to see some really gruesome archaeological findings, look up what it meant for the Babylonians or Chaldeans to conquer a people. I'm not saying what they did to the people they conquered because I don't want to leave people here trying to get disturbing images out of people's minds, but this was a terrible doomsday prophecy.

The prophet answered the Lord in anguish and asked how a God whose eyes were too pure to look on evil could possibly punish his wicked people by the much more wicked Babylonians. And the Lord's response is very mysterious: "The righteous shall walk by faith."

Let me ask you a question: How is this an answer to what the prophet asked the Lord? Answer: It isn't. It's a refusal to answer. The same thing could have been said by saying, "I AM the Lord, and my thoughts are not your thoughts, nor are my ways your ways. I AM WHO I AM and *I will do what I will do*, and I am sovereign in this. I choose not to tell you how, in my righteousness, I choose to let my wicked children be punished by the gruesomely wicked Babylonians. Only know this: even in these conditions, the righteous shall walk by faith."

The words "The righteous shall walk by faith" are an enigma, a shroud, and a protecting veil. To use them as Paul did is a legitimate use of authority, an authority that can

only be understood from the inside, but these words remain
a protecting veil even as they take on a more active role in
the New Testament. The New Testament assumes the Old
Testament even as the New Testament unlocks the Old
Testament.

Paul does not say, "The righteous will walk by sight,"
even as he invokes the words, "The righteous shall walk by
faith."

Here's something to ponder: The righteous shall walk
by faith even in their understanding of the words, "The
righteous shall walk by faith."

In the Name of the Father, and of the Son, and of the
Holy Ghost. Amen.

When I showed this to one Reformation scholar to check
my treatment of the Reformation, he said that I didn't explain
what "The righteous shall walk by faith," but my entire point was
to show what the Old Testament quotation could mean *besides* a
shibboleth that one is sanctified in entirety in response to faith
without one iota being earned by good works. The Reformation
teaching, as I understand it, reflects a subtle adaptation of the
Pauline usage--and here I might underscore that Paul and Luther
had different opponents--and a profound adaptation of the Old
Testament usage. And it may be possible to properly understand
the Biblical text without interpreting it along Reformation lines.

Sixth, you write that Orthodox tend to have a poor
understanding of sovereign grace. I remember how offended my
spiritual Father was when I shared that a self-proclaimed non-
ordained Reformed minister--the one person who harassed me
when I became Orthodox--said that Orthodox didn't believe in
grace. He wasn't offended at me, but I cannot ever recall seeing
him be more offended. (Note: that harassment was a bitter
experience, but I'd really like to think I'm not bitter towards
Calvinists; I have a lot of fond memories from my time at Calvin
and some excellent memories of friends who tended to be born
and bred Calvinists.)

I would suggest that if you can say that Orthodox do not understand sovereign grace shortly after talking about a heavy emphasis on theosis, you are thinking about Orthodox doctrine through a Western grid and are missing partly some details and partly the big picture of how things fit together.

Seventh, I am slightly surprised that you describe original sin as simply being in the Bible and something Orthodox do not teach. Rom 5:12 as translated in the Vulgate ("...in quo omnes peccaverunt") has a Greek ambiguity translated out, so that a Greek text that could quite justifiably be rendered that death came into the world "because all sinned" (NIV) is unambiguously rendered as saying about Adam, "in whom all have sinned," which in turn fed into Augustine's shaping of the Western doctrine of original sin. It's a little surprising to me that you present this reading of an ambiguity as simply being what the Bible says, so that the Orthodox are deficiently presenting the Bible by not sharing the reading.

Eighth, I too was puzzled by the belief that the Incarnation immediately justifies icons, and I find it less puzzling to hold a more nuanced understanding of the Orthodox teaching that if you understand the Incarnation on patristic terms--instead of by a Reformation definition--its inner logic flows out to the point of an embrace of creation that has room for icons. I won't develop proof-texts here; what I will say is that the kind of logical inference that is made is similar to a kind of logical inference I see in your report, i.e. that "The righteous shall walk by faith" means the Reformation doctrine that we are justified by faith alone and not by works.

I believe that this kind of reasoning is neither automatically right nor automatically wrong, but something that needs to be judged in each case.

Ninth, you write, "Finally, many of the Orthodox tend to have a lower view of the Bible than the ancient Fathers had." When I was about to be received into the Orthodox Church, I told my father that I had been devoted in my reading of the Bible and I would switch to being devoted in my reading of the Fathers. My spiritual father, who is a graduate of St. Vladimir's Seminary, emphatically asked me to back up a bit, saying that the Bible was the core text and the Fathers were a commentary. He's said that he would consider himself very fortunate if his parishioners would spend half an hour a day reading the Bible. On an Orthodox mailing list, one cradle Orthodox believer among mostly converts quoted as emphatic an Orthodox clergyman saying, "If you don't read your Bible each day, you're not a Christian." Which I would take as exaggeration, perhaps, but exaggeration as a means of emphasizing something important.

Tenth, regarding higher-critical views at St. Vladimir's Seminary: I agree that it is a problem, but I would remind you of how St. Vladimir's Seminary and St. Tikhon's Seminary compare. St. Vladimir's Seminary is more liberal, and it is an excellent academic environment that gives degrees including an Orthodox M.Min. St. Tikhon's Seminary is academically much looser but it is considered an excellent preparation for ministry. If you saw some degree of liberal academic theology at St. Vladimir's, you are seeing the fruits of your (legitimate) selection. Not that St. Vladimir's Seminary is the only Orthodox seminary which is not completely perfect, but if you want to see preparation for pastoral ministry placed ahead of academic study at an Orthodox institution, St. Tikhon's might interest you.

Eleventh, after I was at Calvin, I remembered one friend, tongue-in-cheek, talking about "the person who led me to Calvin." I also remember that when I was at Calvin, I heard more talk about being "disciples of John Calvin" than being "disciples of Jesus Christ," and talk more about bearing the name of "Calvinist" than "Christian," although this time it wasn't tongue-in-cheek. I notice that you speak of how, "sadly," people "left the Reformed *faith* for Orthodoxy." One response might be one that Reformers like Calvin might share: "Was John Calvin crucified for you? Or were you baptized in the name of John Calvin?" (Cf I Cor. 1:13)

I left this out at first because it's not as "nice" as some of the others, but I would like to invite you to perhaps leave the "faith" (as you call it) that aims for John Calvin, and embrace the faith that Calvin was trying to re-create in response to abuses in the Western Church. It's still alive, and we still have an open door for you.

A Postmodern-Influenced Conclusion

When I studied early modern era Orthodox Patriarch Cyril Lucaris, I compared the Eucharistic teaching in his profession of faith to the Eucharistic teaching in Calvin's <u>Institutes</u>...

...and concluded that Calvin was more Orthodox. Calvin, among other things, concerned himself with the question of what John Chrysostom taught.

I really don't think I was trying to be a pest. But what I did not develop is that Calvin tried to understand what the Greek Fathers taught, always as an answer to Protestant questions about what, in metaphysical terms, happens to the Holy Gifts. The Orthodox question is less about the transformation of the Holy Gifts than the transformation of those who receive it, and Calvin essentially let the Fathers say whatever they wanted... as long as they answered a question on terms set by the Reformation.

When I read Francis Schaeffer's <u>How Should We Then Live?</u>, my immediate reaction was that I wished the book had been "expanded to six times its present length." I have some reservations about the fruitfulness of presuppositional apologetics now. What I do not have reservations about is saying that there is a valid insight in Schaeffer's approach, and more specifically there is distortion introduced by letting Orthodoxy say whatever it wants... as an answer to Calvinist questions.

To assert, without perceived need for justification, that the Orthodox have very little understanding of sovereign grace and follow this claim by saying that there is a preoccupation with divinization comes across to Orthodox much like saying, "________ have very little concept of 'medicine' or 'health' and are always frequenting doctor's offices, pharmacies, and exercise clubs." It's a sign that Orthodox are allowed to fill in the details of sin, incarnation, justification, or (in this case) grace, but on condition that they are filling out the Reformation's unquestioned framework.

But the way to understand this is less analysis than worship.

Money

Today the biggest symbol of evil is Hitler or Naziism; there is almost no bigger insult than calling someone a Nazi or a comparison to Hitler. The Old Testament's symbol of evil that did the same job was a city in which the Lord God of Hosts could not find fifty righteous, nor forty-five, nor forty, nor thirty, nor twenty, nor even ten righteous men. It was the city on which fire and brimstone rained down from Heaven in divine wrath until smoke arose as from a gigantic furnace. It was, in short, the city of Sodom.

Ezekiel has some remarks about Sodom's sin that might surprise you. Ezekiel 16:49 says, *This was the sin of your sister Sodom: she and her daughters had pride, more than enough food, and prosperous ease, but did not aid the poor and needy.*

These are far from the only stinging words the Bible says to rich people who could care for the poor and do not do so. Jesus said something that could better be translated, "It is easier for a rope to pass through the eye of a needle than for a rich person to enter the Kingdom of God." (Mark 10:25). It would take hours or perhaps days to recite everything blunt the Bible says about wealth, if even I could remember so much.

But who are the rich? The standard American answer is, "People who have more money than I do," and the standard American answer is wrong. It takes too much for granted. Do you want to know how special it is, worldwide, to be able to afford meat for every meal you want it and your Church permits it? Imagine saying "We're not rich; we just have Champagne and lobster every day." That's what it means for even poorer Americans to say "We're not rich, just a bit comfortable." The amount of money that America spends on weight loss products each year costs more than it would cost to feed the hungry worldwide. When Ezekiel says that "your sister Sodom" had more than enough food *but did not care for the poor*, he is saying something that has every relevance to us if we also fail to care for the poor.

I would be remiss not to mention the Sermon on the Mount here, because the Sermon on the Mount explains something we can miss (Matt 6:19-21,24-33):

> Do not lay up for yourselves treasures on earth, where moth and rust consume and where thieves break in and steal, but lay up for yourselves treasures in heaven, where neither moth nor rust consumes and where thieves do not break in and steal. For where your treasure is, there will your heart be also... No man can serve two masters; for either he will hate the one and love the other, or he will be devoted to the one and despise the other. You cannot serve God and Money.
>
> Therefore I tell you, do not worry about your life, what you shall eat or what you shall drink, nor about your body, what you shall put on. Is not life more than food, and the body more than clothing? Look at the birds of the air: they neither sow nor reap nor gather into barns, and yet your heavenly Father feeds them. Are you not of more value than they? Do you think that by worrying you can add a single hour to your life? You might as well try to make yourself a foot taller! And why do you worry about clothing? Consider the lilies of the field, how they grow; they neither toil nor spin; yet I tell you, even Solomon in all his glory was not arrayed one of these. But if God so clothes the grass of the field, which today is alive and tomorrow is thrown into the oven, will he not much more clothe you, O men of little faith? Therefore do not worry,

saying, `What shall we eat?' or `What shall we drink?' or
`What shall we wear?' For the Gentiles seek all these things;
and your heavenly Father knows that you need them all. But
seek first the Kingdom of God and his perfect
righteousness, and all these things shall be added unto you.

This *includes* a hard saying about wealth, but it is not only a
hard saying about wealth, but an invitation to joy. "Do not store
up treasures on earth but store up treasures in Heaven" is a
command to exchange lead for gold and have true wealth. It is an
invitation to joy, and it is no accident that these sharp words about
Money lead directly into the Bible's central text on why we never
need to worry.

Elsewhere we read, "A man's life does not consist in the
abundance of his possessions," (Luke 12:15), which is *not* a
statement that spiritual people can rise so high that *their* lives
aren't measured by possessions. It is about everybody, great and
small. If money doesn't make you happy this is not something
specially true about spiritual people; it's something that's true of
everybody. But Jesus's entire point is to direct us to what our life
does consist in. The words about storing up treasures in Heaven
prepare us for the "*Therefore* I tell you," and an invitation to live a
life that is fuller, richer, more vibrant, deeper, more alive, more
radiant with the light of Heaven than we can possibly arrange
through wealth.

What will we leave behind if we spend less on ourselves?
Will we leave behind the Lord's providence, or hugs, or
friendship, or banter, or worship, or the Church, or feasting? Will
we leave behind the love of the Father, or Christ as our High
Priest, or the Spirit? Will we be losing a Heaven whose beginning
is here and now, or will we be pulling out our right hands and our
right eyes? If it seems that way, we may adapt C.S. Lewis to say
that living the life of Heaven through our finances today may
seem like it will cost our right hand and our right eye, or in
today's words an arm and a leg, but once we have taken that
plunge, we will discover that what we have left behind is

precisely nothing. Or perhaps we could say that we are leaving behind a false Savior who never delivers, but only distracts us from the true Savior in Christ, and the treasure that is ours when we lay our treasures at his feet.

Is there a luxury you could give up in this invitation to joy?

The Christmas Tales

Prologue

Another gale of laughter shook the table. "But it always seems like this," Father Bill said. "The time for fasting has passed, and now we are ready to feast. People melt away from the parish hall to enjoy Christmas together, and there is finally one table. Outside, the snow is falling... falling... wow. That's some heavy snowfall."

Adam looked around. "Hmm... That car in the street is having trouble... Ok, it's moving again. I wouldn't want to be driving home in this snow."

Mary smiled. "Why don't we go around the circle, and each tell a story, or share something, or... something? I think we're going to be here for a while."

And so the stories began.

Innocent's Tale: The Apostle

Innocent said, "I was visiting with my nephew Jason, and he asked me, 'Why are you called Innocent now, or Uncle Innocent, or whatever?' I told him that I was named after one of the patron saints of America, called Apostle to America.

"He said, 'Patron saint of America? I bet he wasn't even an American! And I bet you're going to tell me his boring life!'

"I smiled, and said, 'Sit down, kid. I'm going to bore you to tears.'"

And this is how he tried to bore Jason to tears.

Where should I start? He was born just before 1800 into the family of a poor sexton. Stop laughing, Jason, that means a church's janitor. The saint was reading the Bible in church at the age of six--the age he was orphaned at. He went to seminary, and aside from being the top pupil in everything from theology and rhetoric to languages, he was popular with the other seminarians because he invented a pocket sundial, and everybody wanted one. This wasn't our time, you couldn't buy a digital watch, and... I think that was cool. He loved to build things with his hands--later on, he built a church with his own hands, and he built a clock in the town hall of--I forget where, but it's in Alaska, and it's still working today. He would also teach people woodworking. So he was a tinkerer and an inventor. Among other things. Among many other things. At school, he learned, and learned, and learned-- Slavonic, Latin, Greek, for instance, if you wanted to look at languages. At least that's what he learned at school. That doesn't count the dozen or two languages he learned when he got out into the world and started to travel--his version of courtesy seemed to include learning people's languages when he traveled to their countries.

He was a bit of a Renaissance man. But he did more than languages. His biggest gifts were his humility, patience, and love for all people, but if we forget those, he had a spine of solid steel. He became a deacon and then a priest, and his wife broke down in tears when the bishop asked for someone to go to the terrifying and icy land of Alaska and he was the one volunteer for it. This man, who was not afraid of Siberia, was not afraid of Alaska either, and later on, when he became a bishop, he thought it was a bishop's duty to visit all the parishes he was responsible for, and so would travel to all the parishes, by reindeer, by kayak, by dogsled. This wasn't just cool that he could travel different ways. He would carry his little boat... and kayak up rivers of icewater... when he was 60. Yes, 60. This super hero was real.

He traveled a lot, and met peoples, and understood their

languages and cultures. Back when Western missionaries were teaching Africans that they had to become European to be Christian, he came to people, learned their languages, and tried to model Christ's incarnation by taking the flesh of their culture. There were some things he changed--he stopped child sacrifice--but, well, let me think. He did teach woodworking, and he gave the Aleuts a written language. But he never tried to make the people into copies of himself. And he was a very effective evangelist. He learned the dialects and languages of Aleutians, Koloshes, Kurils, Inuit, Kenai, Churgaches, Kamchadals, Oliutores, Negidates, Samogirs, Golds, Gulyaks, Koryaks, Tungus, Chukcha, Yakutians, and Kitians. And he wrote grammars for some of their languages, and his ethnographic, geographic, and linguistic works got him elected an honorary member of the Russian Geographical Society and Moscow Royal University.

What does this have to do with America? Jason, our country is bigger than just white people. Now we think of "bigger than white people" as recognizing how fortunate we are to have blacks, Asians, and Hispanics. But a lot of people in Alaska aren't white. The first nations didn't get exterminated. Saint Innocent is a large part of why the original Americans are to this day known to be over a third Orthodox. And Saint Innocent was elected Bishop of China--sorry, I forgot about that--and he also wanted a diocese for America, and wanted everything to be in English. He created written service books and translated part of the Bible for the Aleuts, and he had a sort of vision for an American Orthodox Church. If you don't believe me that he has something to do with America, and you don't count his extensive work in Alaska and beyond, you can at least take the U.S. Government's word for it when they made him an honorary U.S. Citizen. What's so special about that? Well, let me list all the other people in our nation's history who've been granted that honor. There's Winston Churchill, and the Marquis de LaFayette, and... as far as I know, that's it. Jason, you know about the Congressional Medal of Honor? Being made an honorary citizen is much rarer than that!

After all these things, he was made Patriarch of Moscow--
one of the top five bishops of the world, with huge responsibility.
And after all he had done, and with the new responsibility that
had been given to him... He was basically the Orthodox President
of the United States, and he still kept an open door. Anyone, just
anyone, could come and talk with him. And whoever it was,
whatever the need was, he always did something so that the
person walked out... taken care of. Now it's not just amazing that
there was one person who could do all of these things. It's
amazing that there was one person who could do *any* of these
things.

Is your Mom here already? I haven't talked about the
humanitarian work he did, how when he came to power he
worked hard to see that the poor and needy were cared for. I
haven't talked about what it was like for Russians to be at the
Alaskan frontier--they called it, not West, but the utter East. And
it attracted some pretty weird customers. I haven't talked about
the other saints he was working with--Saint Herman, for instance,
who defended people against Russian frontiersmen who would
kill them, and baked biscuits for children, and wore chains and
dug a cave for himself with his hands, and... um... thanks for
listening.

Just remember, this is one of the saints who brought
Orthodoxy to America.

Mary's Tale: Mary's Treasures

John finally spoke. "What's that you're humming, Mary? A
penny for your thoughts."

Mary continued humming for a moment, and then sung, in a
far-off, dreamy, sing-song voice,

Raindrops on roses,
And whiskers on kittens,
Bright copper kettles,
And warm woolen mittens,

Brown paper packages,
Tied up with strings...

"I was just thinking about what I have to be thankful for,
about a few of my favorite things."
Her husband Adam held out his hand. "What are they?"
She slipped her hand into his. "Well..."

I am thankful for my husband Adam, the love of my life. He
is a servant to God, the best husband in the world to me, and the
best father in the world to our daughter Barbara.

I am thankful for my mother. She is practical and wise. She
is also beautiful. If you think I am pretty, you have seen nothing
of the loveliness etched into her face, the treasure map of wrinkles
around her kind, loving eyes. She taught me... I don't know how
to tell you all the things she taught me. And I am fortunate to have
my mother and her mother alive.

My grandmother... When I close my eyes, I can still smell
her perfume. I can walk through her garden and see the ivy
climbing on the trees, the wild flowers roosting. She thinks her
garden has lost what she used to give it. I only see... I don't know
how to describe it.

I am thankful for my father. He was a gruff man with a
heart of gold. I still remember how every Christmas, as long as he
was alive, he gave me a present carved out of wood.

I am thankful for my daughter Barbara, the other love of my
life. I remember how, it was only this year, she asked for some
money to go shopping at school, where they have a little market
where you can spend $2.00 for a bottle of perfume that smells... to
put it delicately, it hints at a gas station. I gruffly said that there
were better ways to spend money, and that if she really needed
something, she had her allowance. That day I was cleaning her
room, and saw her piggy bank empty. She came back after lunch
and said, "I have a present for you." I looked, and saw a bottle of
perfume. That bottle is on the shelf for my best perfumes, because
it's too precious for me to wear when she doesn't ask me to.

I am thankful for the flowers I can grow in my garden.

Right now it looks nothing like my grandmother's garden. I still hope I'll learn to make a garden beautiful without neat little rows, but for now I work hard to see the flowers in neat little rows.

I am thankful for God, and for *metanoia*, repentance. There was something I was struggling with yesterday, a cutting word I spoke, and I was terrified of letting it go, then when I did... it was... Repenting is the most terrifying experience before and the most healing after. Before you're terrified of what will happen if you let go of something you can't do without, then you hold on to it and struggle and finally let go, and when you let go you realize you were holding onto a piece of Hell. I am thankful for a God who wants me to let go of Hell.

I'm thankful for wine. That one doesn't need explaining.

I'm thankful for babies. It's so nice to hold my friends' babies in my arms.

I'm thankful for--if you go to the <u>Orthodox Church in America</u> website at <u>oca.org</u> and click on <u>Feasts and Saints of the Church</u> followed by <u>Lives of the Saints</u>, there are the lives of many saints. There's a whole world to explore, and it's fascinating to see all the women to look up to. I'm not saying I could measure up to any of them, but... it's something to read, even if I couldn't be like any of them.

I'm thankful for Beethoven's moonlight sonata. Every time I hear it, it's like a soft blue fog comes rolling in, and I'm in a stone hut in the woods lit by candlelight, and I can see the softness all around me. I can feel the fur of the slippers around my feet as I dance in the woods, and I can feel the arms of the one I love wrapped around me.

I'm thankful for all of my husband's little kindnesses.

I'm thankful I didn't run out of any office supplies this week.

I'm thankful our car hasn't broken down this month. We've gotten more mileage out of it than we should have. but we can't afford a new one.

I'm thankful that all of the people in my family, near and far, are in really good health.

I'm thankful that Adam screws the cap onto the toothpaste and always leaves the toilet seat down.

I'm thankful that April Fool's Day only comes once a year. Believe me, in this family, once a year is plenty!

I'm glad that the Orthodox Church is alive and growing.

I'm thankful for all the dirty laundry I have to do. We have dirty laundry because we have enough clothes, and we have dirty dishes because we have food.

I'm glad that Barbara has helped me make bread and cookies ever since she was big enough to stand and drool into the mixing bowl.

I'm profoundly grateful my husband doesn't make me read the books he likes.

I'm glad Adam always remembers to bring a half-gallon of milk home when I ask him, even if he's had a busy day.

I'm glad that when Adam comes home, he asks me to tell him everything that happened in my day, so that I can help him concentrate on what he's thinking about.

I'm thankful that Adam doesn't criticize me when I know I'm wrong, and never humiliates me.

I'm glad that Adam doesn't stick his thumb in my eye like he did when we were dating, and sometimes he doesn't even step on my foot when we dance together... and *sometimes* he doesn't even--*Ow!* Ok, ok! I won't tell that one!

Let's see. This is getting to be all about Adam. I really appreciate having confession, where you let go of sin and it is obliterated. I appreciate how the worship at church flows like a creek, now quick, now slow, now turning around in eddies. I appreciate that our parish is more than a social hub, but it's a place I can connect with people. And I appreciate... let me take a breath...

Mary dimpled. "And..." She squeezed Adam's hand. "There's one more thing. Thank you for praying and keeping us in your prayers for well over a year. We're expecting another child." She blushed and looked down.

And Mary pondered all these treasures in her heart.

Paul's Tale: Another Kind of Mind

Paul leaned forward and began to tell...

When I was younger, I had the nickname of "The Razor." It seemed like my mind would cut into anything I applied it to. When my friends saw the movie *Dungeons & Dragons*, they were appalled when they asked me for my usual incendiary review and I said, "As far as historical fiction goes, it's better than average." It wasn't just the line where a dwarf told an elf he needed to get a woman who weighed two hundred and fifty pounds and had a beard he could hang on to--that single line gave an encounter with another culture that is awfully rare in a classic like *The Witch of Blackbird Pond*. I had liked the beginning impassioned "How dare you fail to see that everybody's equal?" Miss America-style "I get my opinions from *Newsweek*" speech about the evils of having a few elite magi rule. That was mercifully hitting you on the head with something that's insidious in most historical fiction--namely, that the characters are turn-of-the-millennium secular people in armor, conceived without any empathy for the cultures they're supposed to represent. It had the courtesy not to convince you that that's how medievals thought. Plus the movie delivered magic, and impressive sights, and people who enjoyed the benefits of modern medicine and diet, a completely inappropriate abundance of wealth, and everything else we expect in historical fiction. The movie is clumsily done, and its connection to the medieval way of life is tenuous, but it has a pulse. It delivers an encounter that most viewers weren't expecting. Namely, it provides an encounter how D&D is played--despite what some critics say, it's not a botched version of "Hollywood does fantasy", but a good rendering, even a nostalgic rendering, of a rather uninspired D&D session. And at least for that reason, it has a pulse where most historical fiction doesn't. As far as a seed for discussion goes, I said I'd rather start with *Dungeons & Dragons* than with most of the historical fiction I know of.

I was known for using the term 'assassin's guild' to refer to any organization that derived profit from causing people's deaths. This meant not only a cigarette manufacturer like Phillip Morris, or Planned Parenthood, but included more respected organizations like Coca-Cola, which murdered South American unionizers, or department stores, where human blood was the price paid to offer items so cheap. I'm sure you've seen the email forward about what happened when a young man asked Nike to sell him a pair of shoes with the word "sweatshop" on the side. There are disturbingly many things like that that happen, and I was acute at picking them out.

So D&D and the assassin's guild represent two of the things I could observe, and I observed a great deal of them. Wherever I placed the cynic's razor, it would slice. I was adept at cutting. No one could really stand against me.

I still remember a conversation with one friend, Abigail. She said to me, "I don't doubt that everything that you see is there." Abigail paused, and said, "But is it good for you to look at all that?" I remembered then that I gave her a thousand reasons why her question was missing the point, and the only response she made: "Have you ever tried looking for good?"

I had no response to that, and I realized that the back edge of the razor was dull when I tried to look for good. I looked and I saw evil, but it was years of work before I could perceive the good I never looked for. Earlier I thought that politeness was in very large measure a socially acceptable place to deceive; now I saw that ordinary politeness, such as I used to scorn, had more layers consideration and kindness that I would have ever guessed.

Some years later, I met with an Orthodox priest, and we began to talk. It was Fr. Michael; you know him, and how he welcomes you. After some time, I said, "You don't know how much better it is now that I am using my intellect to perceive good." He looked at me and said, "What would you say if I told you that you don't even know what your intellect is?"

I looked at him. "Um... I have no place to put that suggestion. What do you mean?"

He closed his eyes in thought. "You're a bookish fellow. Have you read Descartes, or the Enlightenment's enthronement of reason, or even the popularizations of science that good scientists wince at?"

I said, "A little."

He said, "I think you mean yes."

I tried not to smile.

He continued, "Read Plato for something that's a little saner. Then read John Chrysostom and Maximus Confessor. Try on the difference between what they say about the mind."

I said, "I'm sure I'll find interesting nuances on the concept of mind."

Before leaving, he said, "So long as you've found only nuances on a concept of mind, you have missed the point."

That remark had my curiosity, if nothing else, and so I began to read. I began trying to understand what the different nuances were on the concept of mind, and... It was a bit like trying to mine out the subtle nuances between the word 'Turkey' when it means a country and 'turkey' when it meant a bird.

When someone like John Chrysostom or Maximus Confessor talks about the "intellect," you're setting yourself up not to understand if you read it as "what IQ is supposed to measure." Intellect *does* mean mind, but in order to understand what that means, you have to let go of several things you don't even know you assume about the mind.

If you look at the vortex surrounding Kant, you think that there's a real outer world, and then we each have the private fantasies of our own minds. And the exact relation between the fixed outer world and the inner fantasy varies; modernism focuses on the real outer world and postmodernism on the private inner fantasy, but they both assume that when you say "inner" you must mean "private."

But what Maximus Confessor, for instance, believed, was that the inner world was an inner world of spiritual realities--one could almost say, "not your inner world, not my inner world, but *the* inner world." Certainly it would seem strange to say that my inner world is my most private possession, in a sense even stranger than saying, "My outer world is my most private possession." And if you can sever the link between "inner" and "private," you have the first chink between what the intellect could be besides another nuance on reason.

Out of several ways that one could define the intellect, one that cuts fairly close to the heart of it is, "Where one meets God." The intellect is first and foremost the spiritual point of contact, where one meets God, and that flows into meeting spiritual realities. Thought is a matter of meeting these shared realities, not doing something in your mind's private space. The intellect is mind, but most of us will have an easier time understanding it if we start from the spirit than if we start at our understanding of mind.

The understanding of knowledge is very different if you have a concept of the intellect versus having a concept of the reason. The intellect's knowing is tied to the body and tied to experience. It has limitations the reason doesn't have: with reason you can pick anything up that you have the cleverness for, without needing to have any particular character or experience. If you're sharp, you can pick up a book and have the reason's knowledge. But the intellect knows by sharing in something, knows by drinking. Someone suggested, "The difference between reason and intellect, as far as knowledge goes, is the difference between knowing about your wife and knowing your wife." The reason knows *about* the things it knows; the intellect knows *of* things, by tasting, by meeting, by experiencing, by sharing, by loving.

And here I am comparing the intellect and the reason on reason's grounds, which is the way to compare them as two distinct concepts but not to meet them with the deepest part of your being. We know Christ when we drink his body and blood. Something of the intellect's knowing is why words for "know" are the main words for sexual union in the Bible: "Now Adam knew Eve his wife", and things like that. While the reason puts things together,by reasoning from one thing to another, the intellect *sees,* and knows as the angels know, or as God knows.

And when I asked him, "When can I learn more of this?" Fr. Michael said, "Not from any book, at least not for now. Come, join our services, and they will show you what books cannot." I was startled by the suggestion, but Orthodox worship, and the Orthodox Way, gave me something that Maximus Confessor's confusing pages could not. The concept of the intellect does not appear as a bare and obscure theory in Orthodoxy any more than the concept of eating; people who have never heard of the 'intellect', under any of its names, are drawn to know the good by it. It's like a hiker who sees beauty on a hike, strives to keep going, and might have no idea she's getting exercise.

The lesson I'm now learning could be narrowly stated as "Theology is not philosophy whose subject-matter is God." I pretended to listen politely when I heard that, but philosophy is reason-knowing and theology is intellect-knowing. It's unfortunate that we use the same word, "know," for both. Christ said, "Seek first the Kingdom of Heaven, and all these things shall be added to you." Originally he was talking about food and drink, but I've come to taste that "all these things" means far more. I sought a knowledge of the good, and so I was trying to think it out. Since I've begun to walk the Orthodox Way, as how God wants me to seek the Kingdom of Heaven, I've tasted good in ways I would never have imagined. When I first spoke with Fr. Michael, I was hoping he would give me more ideas I could grasp with my reason. Instead he gave me an invitation to step into a whole world of wonder I didn't know was open to me, and to enter not with my reason alone but with my whole life.

When we worship, we use incense. I am still only beginning to appreciate that, but there is prayer and incense ascending before God's throne, and when we worship, it is a beginning of Heaven. When the priest swings the censer before each person, he recognizes the image of Christ in him. When we kiss icons, whether made of wood or flesh, our display of love and reverence reaches God. Our prayer is a participation in the life of the community, in the life of Heaven itself. We are given bread and wine, which are the body and blood of Christ, and we drink nothing less than the divine life from the fountain of immortality. Christ became what we are that we might become what he is. The Son of God became a Man and the Son of Man that men might become gods and the sons of God. And we live in a world that comprehends the visible and invisible, a world where spirit, soul, and matter interpenetrate, where we are created as men and women, where eternity breathes through time, and where every evil will be defeated and every good will be glorified.

And there is much more to say than that, but I can't put it in words.

John's Tale: The Holy Grail

Mary looked at John and said, "Have you read *The da Vinci Code*?" She paused, and said, "What did you think of it?"

John drew a deep breath.

Mary winced.

John said, "The Christians I know who have read *The da Vinci Code* have complained about what it presents as history. And most of the history is... well, only a couple of notches higher than those historians who claim the Holocaust didn't happen. I personally find picking apart *The da Vinci Code*'s historical inaccuracies to be distasteful, like picking apart a child's toy. Furthermore, I think those responses are beside the point."

Mary said, "So you think the history is sound?"

John said, "I think that a lot of people who think they're convinced by the history in *The da Vinci Code* have been hoodwinked into thinking it's the history that persuaded them. *The da Vinci Code*'s author, Dan Brown, is a master storyteller and showman. *The da Vinci Code* isn't a compelling book because someone stuck history lectures in a bestseller. *The da Vinci Code* is a compelling book because it sells wonder. Dan Brown is the kind of salesman who could sell shoes to a snake, and he writes a story where Jesus is an ordinary (if very good) man, is somehow more amazing of a claim that Jesus is the person where everything that was divine met everything that was human.

"*The da Vinci Code* boils down to a single word, and that word is 'wonder.' Dan Brown, as the kind of person who can sell shoes to a snake, leaves the reader with the distinct impression that the ideas he is pushing are more exotic, alluring, and exciting than the Christianity which somehow can't help coming across as a blob of dullness."

Mary said, "But don't you find it an exciting book? Something which can add a bit of spice to our lives?"

John said, "It is an excellent story--it gripped me more than any other recent bestseller I've read. It is captivating and well-written. It has a lot of excellent puzzles. And its claim is to add spice to our lives. That's certainly what one would expect. But let's look at what it dismisses as ho-hum. Let's look at the Christianity that's supposed to be boring and need a jolt of life from Brown."

Mary said, "I certainly found what Brown said about Mary Magdalene to be an eye-opener. Certainly better than..."

John said, "If I found the relics of Mary Magdalene, I would fall before them in veneration. Mary Magdalene was equal to the twelve apostles--and this isn't just my private opinion. The Orthodox Church has officially declared her to be equal to the twelve apostles. Matthew, Mark, and Luke all list her first among women who followed Christ to the cross, and John lists her as the one who first saw the secret of the resurrection. She has her own feast day, July 22, and it's a big enough feast that we celebrate the Eucharist that day. Tradition credits her with miracles and bold missionary journeys. The story is told of her appearing before the Roman Emperor proclaiming the resurrection, and the Emperor said, 'That's impossible. For a man to rise from the dead is as impossible as for an egg to turn red!' Mary Magdalene picked up an egg, and everyone could see it turn red. That why we still give each other eggs dyed red when we celebrate the Lord's resurrection. There are some ancient Christian writings that call Mary Magdalene the Apostle to the Apostles, because it was she herself who told the Apostles the mystery of the resurrection."

Mary said, "Wow." She closed her eyes to take it in, and then said, "Then why did the Catholic Church mount such a smear campaign against her?"

John said, "I said I didn't want to scrutinize *The da Vinci Code*'s revision of history, but I will say that Brown distorts things, quite intentionally as far as I know. And he counts on you, the reader, to make a basic error. Brown is working hard to attack Catholicism--or at least any form of Catholicism that says something interesting to the modern world. *Therefore* (we are supposed to assume) Catholicism is duty-bound to resist whatever Brown is arguing for. Catholicism isn't an attempt to keep its own faith alive. It's just a reaction against Brown.

"Putting it that way makes Brown sound awfully egotistical. I don't think Brown has reasoned it that consistently, or that he thought we might reason it that consistently, but Brown does come awfully close in thinking that if he's pushing something, Rome opposes it. He extols Mary Magdalene, so Rome must be about tearing her down. He glorifies a mysterious place for the feminine, so Rome must be even more misogynistic than the stereotype would have it. I hate to speak for our neighbors at the Catholic parish down the street, but--"

Mary interrupted. "But don't you find something romantic, at least, to think that Mary held the royal seed in her womb?"

John said, "The symbol of the chalice... the womb as a cup... I do find it romantic to say that Mary held the royal seed in her womb. And it's truer than you think. I believe that Mary was the urn that held the bread from Heaven, that she was the volume in which the Word of Life was inscribed, that her womb is more spacious than the Heavens. Only it's a different Mary than you think. I'm not sure how much you know about angels, but there are different ranks, and the highest ranks were created to gaze on the glory of God. The highest two ranks are the cherubim and seraphim, and the cherubim hold all manner of wisdom and insight, while the seraphim burn with the all-consuming fire of holiness. There is no angel holier than these. It is of this different Mary that we sing,

More honorable than the cherubim,
And more glorious beyond compare than the
seraphim,
In virginity you bore God the Word;
True Mother of God, we magnify you.

"Her womb, we are told, is more spacious than the Heavens because it contained uncontainable God. It is the chalice which held something which is larger than the universe, and that is why it is more spacious than the Heavens.

"I reread *The da Vinci Code*, and I don't remember if there was even a passing reference to the other Mary. This seems a little strange. If you're interested in a womb that held something precious, if you're interested in a woman who can be highly exalted, she would seem an obvious choice. I don't think *The da Vinci Code* even raises her as an alternative to refute.

"Not even Dan Brown, however, can get away with saying that the Catholic Church ran a smear campaign against Our Lady. He may be able to sell shoes to snakes, but thanks in part to the Reformation's concern that the Catholic Church was in fact worshipping Mary as God, that's almost as tough a sell as stating that the Catholic Church doesn't believe in God. We Orthodox give Mary a place higher than any angel, and it's understandable for Protestants to say that must mean we give her God's place-- Protestants don't have any place that high for a creature. The Catholic Church, like the Orthodox Church, has a cornucopia of saints, a glorious and resplendent plethora, a dazzling rainbow, and it's possible not to know about the glory of Mary Magdalene. So Brown can sell the idea that the Catholic Church slandered one of her most glorious saints, and... um... quietly hope he's distracted the reader from the one woman whom no one can accuse the Catholic Church of slandering."

Mary looked at him. "There still seemed to be... There is a wonder that would be taken away by saying that Mary Magdalene was not the chalice that held the blood."

John said, "What if I told you that that was a smokescreen, meant to distract you from the fact that wonder was being taken away?"

"Look at it. *The da Vinci Code* has a bit of a buildup before it comes to the 'revelation' that the Grail is Mary Magdalene."

Mary said, "I was curious."

John said, "As was I. I was wishing he would get out and say it instead of just building up and building up. There is a book I was reading--I won't give the author, because I don't want to advertise something that's spiritually toxic--"

Mary smiled. "You seem to be doing that already."

John groaned. "Shut up. I don't think any of you haven't had ads for *The da Vinci Code* rammed down your throat, nor do I think any of you are going to run and buy it to learn about pure and pristine Gnos-- er... Christianity. So just shut up."

Mary stuck out her tongue.

John poked her, and said, "Thank you for squeaking with me.

"Anyway, this book pointed out that the Holy Grail is not a solid thing. It is a shadow. It's like the Cross: the Cross is significant, not just because it was an instrument of vile torture, but because it was taken up by the Storm who turned Hell itself upside-down. Literature has plenty of magic potions and cauldrons of plenty, but all of these pale in comparison with the Holy Grail. That is because the Holy Grail exists in the shadow of an even deeper mystery, a mystery that reversed an ancient curse. Untold ages ago, a serpent lied and said, 'Take, eat. You will not die.' Then the woman's offspring who would crush the serpent's head said, 'Take, eat. You will live.' And he was telling the truth, and he offered a life richer and deeper than anyone could imagine.

"And so there is a mystery, not only that those in an ancient time could eat the bread and body that is the bread from Heaven and drink the wine and blood that is the divine life, but that this mystery is repeated every time we celebrate it. We are blinded to the miracle of life because it is common; we are blinded to this sign because it is not a secret. And it is a great enough miracle that the chalice that held Christ's blood is not one item among others; it is the Holy Grail.

"In the ancient world, the idea that God could take on a body was a tough pill to swallow. It still is; that God should take on our flesh boggles the mind. And there were a lot of people who tried to soften the blow. And one of the things they had to neutralize, in their barren spirituality, was the belief that Christ could give his flesh and blood. The legend of the Holy Grail is a testimony to the victory over that belief, the victory of God becoming human that we might become like him and that he might transform all of our humanity. It says that the cup of Christ, the cup which held Christ's blood, is a treasure because Christ's blood is a treasure, and the image is powerful enough that... We talk about 'Holy Grail's, as in 'A theory that will do this is the Holy Grail of physics.' That's how powerful it is.

"I would say that there were people in the ancient world who didn't get it. In a real sense, Dan Brown picks up where they left off. And part of what he needs to do is make Mary Magdalene, or some substitute, the Holy Grail, because we can't actually have a cup that is the Holy Grail, because we can't actually have a Table where Christ's body and blood are given to all his brothers and sisters.

"And that is the meaning of Mary Magdalene as the Holy Grail. She is a beautiful diversion so we won't see what is being taken away. She is a decoy, meant to keep our eyes from seeing that any place for the Eucharist is vanishing. And I'm sure Mary Magdalene is rolling over in her reliquary about this.

"But in fact the Eucharist is not vanishing. It's here, and every time I receive it, I reverently kiss a chalice that is an image of the Holy Grail. What Dan Brown builds up to, as an exciting revelation, is that Jesus left behind his royal bloodline. This bloodline is alive today, and we see something special when Sophie wraps her arms around the brother she thought was dead. And that is truer than Dan Brown would ever have you guess.

"Jesus did leave behind his blood; we receive it every time we receive the Eucharist. And it courses through our veins. You've heard the saying, 'You are what you eat.' You do not become steak by eating steak, but you do become what Jesus is by eating his flesh. Augustine said, 'See what you believe. Become what you behold.' That's part of the mystery. In part through the Eucharist, we carry Christ's blood. It courses through our veins. And it's not dilute beyond measure, as Dan Brown's picture would have it. We are brothers and sisters to Christ and therefore to one another. There is an embrace of shared blood at the end of *The da Vinci Code*, and there is an embrace, between brothers and sisters who share something much deeper than physical blood, every time we share the holy kiss, or holy hug or whatever. Is the truth as wild as what Dan Brown says? It's actually much wilder."

Mary said, "I can't help feeling that *The da Vinci Code* captures something that... their talk of knights and castles, a Priory that has guarded a secret for generations, a pagan era before the testosterone poisoning we now call Christianity..."

John smiled. "Yes. It had that effect on me too. These things speak of something more. When I was younger, one of my friends pointed out to me that when I said 'medieval', I was referring to something more than the Middle Ages. It was a more-than-literal symbol, something that resonated with the light behind the Middle Ages. And the same is happening with the golden age Brown evokes. All of us have a sense that there is an original good which was lost, or at least damaged, and the yearning Brown speaks to is a real yearning for a legitimate good. But as to the specific golden age... Wicca makes some very specific claims about being the Old Religion that Wiccans resume after the interruption of monotheism. Or at least it made them, and scholars devastated those claims. There are a few Wiccans who continue to insist that they represent the Old Religion instead of a modern Spiritualist's concoction. But most acknowledge that the account isn't literally true: they hold the idea of an 'Old Religion' as an inspiring tale, and use the pejorative term 'Wiccan Fundamentalists' for people who literally believe that Wicca is the Old Religion.

"And so we can yearn for a Golden Age when people

believed the spirit of our own age... um... how can I explain this. People who yearn for an old age when men and women were in balance have done little research into the past. People who think the New Testament was reactionary have no idea of a historical setting that makes the New Testament look like it was written by flaming liberals. Someone who truly appreciated the misogyny in ancient paganism would understand that rape could not only be seen as permissible; quite often it was simply seen as a man's prerogative. Trying to resurrect ancient paganism because Christian views on women bother you is like saying that your stomach is ill-treated by your parents' mashed potatoes so you're going to switch to eating sticks and gravel.

"But I'm getting into something I didn't want to get into...

"There is something from beyond this world, something transcendent, that is shining through Brown's writing. The Priory is haunting. The sacred feminine is haunting. There is something shining through. There is also something shining through in Orthodoxy. And that something is something that has shone through from the earliest times.

"In *The da Vinci Code*, knighthood is a relic of what it used to be. Or at least the knight they visit is a relic, more of a tip of the hat to ages past than a breathing tradition. The Knights Templar at least represent something alive and kicking. They're a society that continues alive today and is at once medieval and modern. They bear the glory of the past, but they bear it today. In that sense they're a glimmer of what the Church is--a society alike ancient and modern, but I'm getting ahead of myself.

"What I meant to be saying is that knighthood is more a tip of the hat than something alive. I've read the Grail legends in their medieval forms, and I've met knights and ladies in those pages. It takes some time to appreciate the medieval tradition--there is every reason for a modern reader to say that the texts are long and tedious, and I can't quickly explain why that understandable reaction is missing something. The knights and ladies there aren't a tip of the hat; they're men and women and they kick and breathe. And they represent something that the medieval authors would never have realized because they had never been challenged. They represent the glory of what it means to be a man, and the glory of what it means to be a woman. We speak of the New Eve, Mary, as 'the most blessed and glorious Lady;' we are called to be a royal priesthood, and when we receive the Eucharist we are called 'the servant of God Adam' or 'the handmaiden of God Eve'--which is also meant to be humble, but inescapably means the Knights and Ladies serving before the King of Kings.

"The Orthodox Church knows a great deal about how to be a knight and how to be a lady. It can be smeared, but it has a positive and distinctive place for both men and women. It may be a place that looks bad when we see it through prejudices we don't realize, but there is a real place for it."

"I know a lot of people who think it's not gender-balanced," Mary said.

John said, "What would they hold as being gender balanced?"

"I'm not sure any churches would be considered gender-balanced."

John said, "All right, which churches come closest?"

Mary said, "Well, the most liberal ones, of course."

John said, "That doesn't mesh with the figures. Men feel out of place in a lot of churches. With Evangelicalism and Catholicism, men aren't that much of a minority, about 45%. Go to the more liberal churches, and you'll find a ratio of about two to one, up to about seven to one. Come to an Orthodox parish, on the other hand, and find men voluntarily attending services that aren't considered mandatory--and the closest to a 50-50 balance in America."

Mary said, "But why? I thought the liberal churches had..."

John interrupted. "What are you assuming?"

Mary answered, "Nothing. Liberal churches have had the most opportunity for women to draw things into a balance."

John continued questioning. "What starting point are you assuming?"

Mary said, "Nothing. Just that things need to be balanced by women... um... just that men have defined the starting point..."

"And?" John said.

Mary continued: "And... um... that women haven't contributed anything significant to the starting point."

John paused. "Rather a dismal view of almost two millennia of contributions by women, don't you think?"

Mary opened her mouth, and closed it. "I need some time to think."

John said, "It took me almost four years to figure it out; I won't fault you if you're wise enough to take some time to ponder it. And I might also mention that the image of being knights and ladies is meant to help understand what it means to be man and woman--*Vive la glorieuse différence!*--and the many-layered mystery of masculinity and femininity, but an image nonetheless. All statements possess some truth, and all statements fall immeasurably short of the truth."

Mary said, "Huh? Are all statements equally true?"

John said, "No. Not all statements are equally true; some come closer to the truth than others. No picture is perfect, but there is such a thing as a more or less complete image. And what I have said about knights and ladies, and many things that could be said about the Church as a society guarding a powerful truth, point to something beyond them. They are great and the truth is greater. There is something in the Priory and the Knights Templar that is poisoned, that infects people with a sweetly-coated pride that ends in a misery that can't enjoy other people because it can't appreciate them, or indeed respect anybody who's not part of the self-same inner ring. That 'inner ring' is in the beginning as sweet as honey and in the end as bitter as gall and as sharp as a double-edged sword, so that struggling to achieve rank in the Priory is a difficult struggle with a bitter end. And in that sense the Priory is an image of the Church... it is a fellowship which has guarded an ancient truth, a truth that must not die, and has preserved it across the ages. But instead of being an inner ring achieved by pride, the Church beckons us to humility. This humility is unlike pride: it is unattractive to begin with, but when we bow we are taller and we find the secret of enjoying the whole universe."

"What is this secret?" Mary asked.

John closed his eyes for a moment and said, "You can only enjoy what you appreciate, and you can only appreciate what you approach in humility. This is part of a larger truth. It takes sobriety to enjoy even drunkenness. If you want to see the one person who cannot enjoy drunkenness, look at an alcoholic. Virtue is the doorway to enjoying everything, even vice.

"There is a treacherous poison beckoning in 'the inner ring', of a secret that is hidden from outsiders one looks down on. The inner ring is a door to Hell."

"You believe that Knights Templar will go to Hell?" Mary said.

John looked at her. "I believe that Knights Templar, and people in a thousand other inner rings, are in Hell already. I don't know how Christ will judge them, but... In the end, some have remarked, there are only two kinds of people: those who tell God, 'Thy will be done,' and those to whom God finally says, '*Thy* will be done.' The gates of Hell are sealed, bolted, and barred from the *inside*, by men who have decided: 'I would rather reign in Hell than serve in Heaven!' In one sense, Hell will never blast its full fury until the Judge returns. In another sense, Hell begins on earth, and the inner ring is one of its gates."

Mary said, "Wow."

John said, "And there is a final irony. What we are led to expect is that there is a great Western illusion. And Brown is going to help us see past it."

Mary said, "And the truth?"

John said, "There is a great Western illusion, and Brown is keeping us from seeing past it.

"There's a rather uncanny coincidence between Brown's version of original, pristine paganism and the fashions feminism happens to take in our day. Our version of feminism is unusual, both in terms of history and in terms of cultures today. It's part of the West that the Third World has difficulty understanding. And yet the real tradition, call it restored paganism or original Christianity or the Old Religion or what have you, turns out to coincide with all the idiosyncracies of our version of feminism. It's kind of like saying that some 1970's archaeologists exhumed an authentic pagan burial site, and it was so remarkably preserved that they could tell the corpses were all wearing bell-bottoms, which was the norm in the ancient world. If we made a statement like that about clothing, we'd need to back it up. And yet Brown does the same sort of thing in the realm of ideas, and it comes across as pointing out the obvious; most people wouldn't think to question him. And this is without reading classical pagan texts about how marriage might lead a man to suicide because of feminine wrangling, and how any man who couldn't deny his wife anything he chose was the lowest of slaves. Brown is a master of showmanship, at helping you see what he wants you to see and not see what he doesn't want you to see.

"If we decline Brown's assistance in seeing past illusions, it turns out that there's another illusion he doesn't help us see past. And, ironically, it is precisely related to symbol.

"Something profound happened in the Middle Ages, or started happening, that is still unfolding today. It is the disenchantment of the entire universe. There are several ways one could describe it. Up until a certain point, everyone took it for granted that horses, people, and colors were all things that weren't originally created in our minds... wait, that was confusing. It's easier to speak of the opposite. The opposite, which began to pick up steam almost a thousand years ago, was that we think up categories like horses and colors, but they don't exist before we think of them. As it would develop, that was a departure from what most people believed. And a seed was planted that would take deeper and deeper root.

"That's the philosophy way of putting it. The symbol's way of putting it is that the departure, the new thinking, drove a wedge between a symbol and what that symbol represented. If you represented something, the symbol was connected to what it represented. That's why, in *The Lord of the Rings*, the hobbits mention Sauron and Gandalf makes a tense remark of, 'Don't mention that name here!'

"Why is this? The name of Sauron was a symbol of Sauron which bore in an invisible way Sauron's presence. When Gandalf told the Hobbits not to mention that name, he was telling them not to bring Sauron's presence."

Mary said, "That sounds rather far-fetched."

John answered, "Would you care to guess why, when you say a friend's name and she stops by, you always say, 'Speak of the Devil!'?"

Mary shifted her position slightly.

John continued. "Those two things are for the same reason. Tolkein was a medievalist who commanded both an excellent understanding of the medieval world, and was steeped in paganism's best heroic literature. He always put me to sleep, but aside from that, he understood the medieval as most modern fantasy authors do not. And when Gandalf commands the hobbits not to speak the name of Sauron, there is a dying glimmer of something that was killed when the West embraced the new way of life."

"The name of something is a symbol that is connected to the reality. Or at least, a lot of people have believed that, even if it seems strange to us. If you read the Hebrew Prophets, you'll find that 'the name of the Lord' is a synonym for 'the Lord' at times, and people write 'the Lord' instead of saying the Lord's actual name: 'the Lord' is a title, like 'the King' or 'the President', not a name like 'Jacob.' People were at first cautious of saying the Lord's name in the wrong way, and by the New Testament most Jews stopped saying the Lord's name at all. This is because people believed a symbol was connected to the reality, and a failure to show proper reverence to the Lord's name was in fact a failure to show proper reverence to the Lord.

"When the Bible says that we are created in the image of God, this is not just a statement that we resemble God in certain ways. It is a statement that God's actual presence operates in each person, and what you do to other people, you cannot help doing to

God. This understanding, too obvious to need saying to the earliest readers, is behind everything from Proverbs' statement that he who oppresses the poor shows contempt for their Maker, to the chilling end of the parable in Matthew 25:

> "When the King returns in glory... he will say to those at his left hand, 'Depart from me, you who are damned, into the eternal fire prepared for the Devil and his angels. For I was hungry and you gave me no food, thirsty and you gave me nothing to drink, a stranger and you did not welcome me, lacking clothes and you did not clothe me, sick and in prison and you did not visit me.' Then they also will answer, 'Lord, when did we see you hungry or thirsty or a stranger or sick or in prison and did not care for you?' Then he will answer them, 'I solemnly tell you, insofar as you did not do it for the least of these brothers of mine, you did not do it for me.'"

Mary thought, and asked, "Do you think that bread and wine are symbols of Christ's body and blood?"

John said, "Yes. I believe they are symbols in the fullest possible sense: bread and wine represent the body and blood of Christ, and *are* the body and blood of Christ. Blood itself is a symbol: the Hebrew Old Testament word for 'blood' means 'life', and throughout the Bible whenever a person says 'shedding blood,' he says, 'taking life.' Not only is wine a symbol of Christ's blood, Christ's blood is a symbol of the uncreated, divine life, and when we drink Christ's blood, we receive the uncreated life that God himself lives. This is the life of which Jesus said, 'Unless you eat the flesh and drink the blood of the Son of Man, you have no life in you.' So the wine, like the bread, is a symbol with multiple layers, Christ's body and blood themselves being symbols, and it is for the sons of God to share in the divine life: to share in the divine life is to be divinized.

"Are these miracles? The question is actually quite deceptive. If by 'miracle' you mean something out of place in the natural order, a special exception to how things are meant to work, then the answer is 'No.'

"The obvious way to try to incorporate these is as exceptions to how a dismembered world works: things are not basically connected, without symbolic resonance, with the special exceptions of the Eucharist and so on. But these are not exceptions. They are the crowning jewel of what orders creation.

"Things are connected; that is why when the Orthodox read the Bible, they see one tree in the original garden with its momentous fruit, and another tree that bore the Son of God as its fruit, and a final tree at the heart of the final Paradise, bearing fruit each season, whose leaves are for the healing of the nations. This kind of resonance is almost as basic as the text's literal meaning itself. Everything is connected in a way the West has lost--and by 'lost', I do not simply mean 'does not have.' People grasp on an intuitive level that symbols have mystic power, or at least should, and so we read about the Knights Templar with their exotic equal-armed crosses, flared at the ends, in red on white. Yes, I know, pretend you don't know there's the same kind of equal-armed cross, flared at the ends, on the backs of our priests and acolytes. The point we're supposed to get is that we need to go to occult symbolism and magic if we are to recover that sense of symbol we sense we have lost, and fill the void.

"But the Orthodox Church is not a way to fill the void after real symbols have been destroyed. Orthodoxy does not need a Harvard 'symbologist' as a main character because it does not need to go to an exotic expert to recover the world of symbol. Orthodoxy in a very real sense has something better than a remedy for a wound it never received.

"To the Orthodox Church, symbols are far more than a code-book, they are the strands of an interconnected web. To the Church, symbols are not desparate escape routes drilled out of prison, but the wind that blows through a whole world that is open to explore."

Mary pondered. "So we have a very deaf man who has said, 'None of us can hear well, so come buy my hearing aid,' and

Orthodox Church as a woman who has never had hearing trouble and asks, 'Why? What would I need one for?'

"And is there something deeper than symbol, even?"

John closed his eyes. "To answer that question, I'm having trouble doing better than paraphrasing Pseudo-Dionysius, and I *wish* we had his *Symbolic Theology.* 'I presume this means something specific. I assume it means that everything, even the highest and holiest things that the eye, the heart... I mean mind... I mean intellect, the intellect which perceives those realities beyond the eye... I mean that everything they can perceive is merely the rationale that presupposes everything below the Transcendent One.'

"Yes, there is One who is deeper than all created symbols."

Basil's Tale: The Desert Fathers

Father Basil said, "When I read the introduction to Helen Waddell's <u>The Desert Fathers</u>, I wasn't disappointed yet. At least, that's where I first met these people; Waddell gives one translation of an ancient collection, and if you search on the Web for *The Sayings of the Desert Fathers*, you can find them easily enough.

"The introduction led me to expect important historical documents in the life of the Church--you know, the sort of first try that's good for you because it's dull and uninteresting, kind of like driving a buggy so you can appreciate what a privilege it is to ride a car. Or like spending a year wasting time on your PC, reinstalling Windows and trying to recover after viruses wreak havoc on your computer, so that when you finally upgrade to a Mac, you appreciate it. Then I actually began to *read* the Desert Fathers, and..."

John asked, "Can you remember any of them? There's..."

Father said, "Yes, certainly."

An old monk planted a piece of dry wood next to a monk's cell in the desert, and told the young monk to water it each day until... So the young monk began the heavy toil of carrying water to water the piece of wood for year after year. After three years, the wood sprouted leaves, and then branches. When it finally bore fruit, the old monk plucked the fruit and said, "Taste the fruit of obedience!"

Three old men came to an old monk, and the last old man had an evil reputation. And the first man told the monk, "Make me a fishing net," but he refused. Then the second man said, "Make me a fishing net, so we will have a keepsake from you," but he refused. Then the third man said, "Make me a fishing net, so I may have a blessing from your hands," and the monk immediately said, "Yes." After he made the net, the first two asked him, "Why did you make him a net and not us?" And he said, "You were not hurt, but if I had said no to him, he would thought I was rejecting him because of his evil reputation. So I made a net to take away his sadness."

A monk fell into evil struggles in one monastery, and the monks cast him out. So he came to an old monk, who received him, and sent him back after some time. But the monks as the monastery wouldn't receive him. Then he sent a message, saying, "A ship was wrecked, and lost all of its cargo, and at last the captain took the empty ship to land. Do you wish to sink on land the ship that was saved from the sea?" Then they received him.

An old monk said, "He who finds solitude and quiet will avoid hearing troublesome things, saying things that he will regret, and seeing temptations. But he will not escape the turmoil of his own heart."

There was a young monk who struggled with lust and spoke to an older monk in desparation. The old monk tore into him, scathing him and saying he was vile and unworthy, and the young monk fled in despair. The young monk met another old monk who said, "My son, what is it?" and waited until the young monk told everything. Then the old monk prayed that the other monk, who had cruelly turned on the young monk, would be tempted. And he ran out of his cell, and the second old monk said, "You have judged cruelly, and you yourself are tempted, and what do you do? At least now you are worthy of the Devil's attention." And the monk repented, and prayed, and asked for a softer tongue.

Once a rich official became a monk, and the priest, knowing he had been delicately raised, sent him such nice gifts as the monastery had been given. As the years passed, he grew in contemplation and in prophetic spirit. Then a young monk came to him, hoping to see his severe ascetic discipline. And he was shocked at his bed, and his shoes, and his clothes. For he was not used to seeing other monks in luxury. The host cooked vegetables, and in the morning the monk went away scandalized. Then his host sent for him, and said, "What city are you from?" "I have never lived in a city." "Before you were a monk, what did you do?" "I cared for animals." "Where did you sleep?" "Under the stars." "What did you eat, and what did you drink?" "I ate bread and had no wine." "Could you take baths?" "No, but I could wash myself in the river." Then the host said, "You toiled before becoming a monk; I was a wealthy official. I have a nicer bed than most monks now. I used to have beds covered with gold; now I have this much cruder bed. I used to have costly food; now I have herbs and a small cup of wine. I used to have many servants; now I have one monk who serves me out of the goodness of his heart. My clothing was once costly beyond price; now you see they are common fare. I used to have minstrels before me; now I sing psalms. I offer to God what poor and feeble service I can. Father, please do not be scandalized at my weakness." Then his guest said, "Forgive me, for I have come from heavy toil into the ease of the monastic life, and you have come from richness into heavy toil. Forgive me for judging you." And he left greatly edified, and would often come back to hear his friend's Spirit-filled words.

A monk came to see a hermit, and when he was leaving, said, "Forgive me, brother, for making you break your monastic rule of solitude." The hermit said, "My monastic rule is to welcome you hospitably and send you away in peace."

Once a group of monks came to an old monk, and another old monk was with them. The host began to ask people, beginning with the youngest, what this or that word in Scripture meant, and each tried to answer well. Then he asked the other old monk, and the other monk said, "I do not know." Then the host said, "Only he has found the road--the one who says, 'I do not know.'"

One old monk went to see another old monk and said to him, "Father, as far as I can I say my handful of prayers, I fast a little, I pray and meditate, I live in peace and as far as I can I purify my thoughts. What else can I do?" Then the old man stood up and stretched his hands towards Heaven. His fingers blazed as ten lamps of fire and he said, "If you desire it, you can become a fire."

A brother asked an old monk, "What is a good thing to do, that I may do it and live?" The old monk said, "God alone knows what is good. Yet I have heard that someone questioned a great monk, and asked, 'What good work shall I do?' And he answered, 'There is no single good work. The Bible says that Abraham was hospitable, and God was with him. And Elijah loved quiet, and God was with him. And David was humble, and God was with him. Therefore, find the desire God has placed in your heart, and do that, and guard your heart."

Macrina's Tale: The Communion Prayer

Mary looked at Macrina. "And I can see you've got something in your purse."

Macrina smiled. "Here. I was just thinking what a blessing it is to have a prayer book. It is a powerful thing to raise your voice with a host of saints, and this version, the Fellowship of St. Alban and St. Sergius's <u>A Manual of Eastern Orthodox Prayers</u>, is my favorite." She flipped a few pages. "This prayer, and especially this version, has held a special place in my heart.

"And... I'm not sure how to put it. Westerners misunderstand us as being the past, but we are living *now*. But in the West, living *now* is about running from the past, trying to live in the future, and repeating the mistakes of the past. Ouch, that came out a lot harsher than I meant. Let me try again... in the East, living now leaves you free to enjoy the glory of the past.

You can learn to use a computer today and still remember how to read books like you were taught as a child. And you are free to keep treasures like this prayer, from St. Simeon the New Theologian ("New" means he died in the 11th century):

From lips besmirched and heart impure,
From unclean tongue and soul sin-stained,
Receive my pleading, O my Christ,
Nor overlook my words, my way
Of speech, nor cry importunate:
Grant me with boldness to say all
That I have longed for, O my Christ,
But rather do thou teach me all
That it behoveth me to do and say.
More than the harlot have I sinned,
Who, learning where thou didst abide,
Brought myrrh, and boldly came therewith
And didst anoint thy feet, my Christ,
My Christ, my Master, and my God:
And as thou didst not cast her forth
Who came in eagerness of heart,
Abhor me not, O Word of God,
But yield, I pray, thy feet to me,
To my embrace, and to my kiss,
And with the torrent of my tears,
As with an ointment of great price,
Let me with boldness them anoint.
In mine own tears me purify,
And cleanse me with them, Word of God,
Remit my errors, pardon grant.
Thou knowest my multitude of sins,
Thou knowest, too, the wounds I bear;
Thou seest the bruises of my soul;
But yet thou knowest my faith, thou seest
My eager heart, and hear'st my sighs.
From thee, my God, Creator mine,

And my Redeemer, not one tear
Is hid, nor e'en the part of one.
Thine eyes mine imperfection know,
For in thy book enrolled ar found
What things are yet unfashioned.
Behold my lowliness, behold
My weariness, how great it is:
And then, O God of all the world,
Grant me release from all my sins,
That with clean heart and conscience filled
With holy fear and contrite soul
I may partake of thy most pure,
Thine holy spotless Mysteries.
Life and divinity hath each
Who eateth and who drinketh thee
Thereby in singleness of heart;
For thou hast said, O Master mine,
Each one that eateth of my Flesh,
And drinketh likewise of my Blood--
He doth indeed abide in me,
And I in him likewise am found.
Now wholly true this saying is
Of Christ, my Master and my God.
For he who shareth in these graces
Divine and deifying is
No wise alone, but is with thee,
O Christ, thou triply-radiant Light,
Who the whole world enlightenest.
Therefore, that I may ne'er abide,
Giver of Life, alone, apart
From thee, my breath, my life, my joy,
And the salvation of the world--
For this, thou seest, have I drawn nigh
To thee with tears and contrite soul;
My errors' ransom to receive
I seek, and uncondemned to share

In thy life-giving Mysteries
Immaculate; that thou mayst dwell
With me, as thou hast promised,
Who am in triple wretchedness;
Lest the Deceiver, finding me
Removed from thy grace by guile
May seize me, and seducing lead
Astray from thy life-giving words.
Wherefore I fall before thy face,
And fervently I cry to thee,
As thou receiv'dst the Prodigal
And Harlot, when she came to thee,
So now my harlot self receive
And very Prodigal, who now
Cometh with contrite soul to thee.
I know, O Savior, none beside
Hath sinned against thee like as I,
Nor done the deeds which I have dared.
But yet again, I know this well,
That not the greatness of my sins,
Nor my transgressions' multitude,
Exceeds my God's forbearance great,
Nor his high love toward all men.
But those who fervently repent
Thou with the oil of lovingness
Dost cleanse, and causest them to shine,
And makest sharers of thy light,
And bounteously dost grant to be
Partakers of thy Divinity;
And though to angels and to minds
Of men alike 'tis a strange thing,
Thou dost converse with them ofttimes--
These thoughts do make me bold, these thoughts
Do give me pinions, O my Christ;
And thus confiding in thy rich
Good deeds toward us, I partake--

Rejoicing, trembling too, at once--
Who am but grass, of fire: and lo!
--A wonder strange!--I am refreshed
With dew, beyond all speech to tell;
E'en as in olden time the Bush
Burning with fire was unconsumed.
Therefore, thankful in mind and heart,
Thankful, indeed, in every limb,
With all my body, all my soul,
I worship thee, yea, magnify,
And glorify thee, O my God,
Both now and to all ages blest.

Barbara's Tale: The Fairy Prince

Adam looked at his daughter and said, "Barbara, what do you have to share? I can hear you thinking."

Barbara looked at her father and said, "You know what I'm thinking, Daddy. I'm thinking about the story you made for me, the story about the fairy prince."

"Why don't you tell it, Sweetie? You know it as well as I do."

The child paused a moment, and said, "You tell it, Daddy."

Here is the tale of the fairy prince.

Long ago and far away, the world was full of wonder. There were fairies in the flowers. People never knew a rift between the ordinary and the magical.

But that was not to last forever. The hearts of men are dark in many ways, and they soon raised their axe against the fairies and all that they stood for. The axe found a way to kill the dryad in a tree but leave the tree still standing--if indeed it was really a tree that was still standing. Thus begun the disenchantment of the entire universe.

Some time in, people realized their mistake. They tried to open their hearts to wonder, and bring the fairies back. They tried to raise the axe against disenchantment--but the axe they were wielding was cursed. You might as well use a sword to bring a dead man to life.

But this story is not about long ago and far away. It is about something that is recent and very near. Strange doings began when the son of the Fairy Queen looked on a world that was dying, where even song and dance and wine were mere spectres of what they had been. And so he disguised himself as a fool, and began to travel in the world of men.

The seeming fool came upon a group of men who were teasing a young woman: not the mirthful, merry teasing of friends, but a teasing of dark and bitter glee. He heard one say, "You are so ugly, you couldn't pay a man enough to kiss you!" She ran away, weeping.

The prince stood before her and said, "Stop." And she looked at him, startled.

He said, "Look at me."

She looked into his eyes, and began to wonder. Her tears stopped.

He said, "Come here."

She stood, and then began walking.

He said, "Would you like a kiss?"

Tears filled her eyes again.

He gave her his kiss.

She ran away, tears falling like hail from her eyes. Something had happened. Some people said they couldn't see a single feature in her face that had changed. Others said that she was radiant. Others still said that whatever she had was better than gorgeous.

The prince went along his way, and he came to a very serious philosopher, and talked with him, and talked, and talked. The man said, "Don't you see? You are cornered. What you are saying is not possible. Do you have any response?"

The prince said, "I do, but it comes not in words, but in an embrace. But you wouldn't be interested in that, would you?"

For some reason, the man trusted him, and something

changed for him too. He still read his books. But he would also dance with children. He would go into the forest, and he did not talk to the animals because he was listening to what the animals had to say.

The prince came upon a businessman, a man of the world with a nice car and a nice house, and after the fairy prince's kiss the man sold everything and gave it away to the poor. He ate very little, eating the poorest fare he could find, and spent much time in silence, speaking little. One of his old friends said, "You have forsaken your treasures!"

He looked at his friend and said, "Forsaken my treasures? My dearest friend, you do not know the beginning of treasure."

"You used to have much more than the beginning of treasure."

"Perhaps, but now I have the greatest treasure of all."

Sometimes the prince moved deftly. He spoke with a woman in the park, a pain-seared woman who decided to celebrate her fiftieth wedding anniversary--or what would have been the fiftieth anniversary of a long and blissful marriage, if her husband were still alive. She was poor, and had only one bottle of champagne which she had been saving for many years. She had many friends; she was a gracious woman. She invited the fairy prince, and it was only much later that her friends began to wonder that that the one small bottle of champagne had poured so amply for each of them.

The prince did many things, but not everybody liked it. Some people almost saw the prince in the fool. Others saw nothing but a fool. One time he went into a busy shopping mall, and made a crude altar, so people could offer their wares before the Almighty Dollar. When he was asked why, he simply said, "So people can understand the true meaning of Christmas. Some people are still confused and think it's a religious holiday." That was not well received.

Not long after, the woman whom he met in the park slept the sleep of angels, and he spoke at her funeral. People cried more than they cried at any other funeral. And their sides hurt. All of this was because they were laughing so hard, and the funny thing was that almost nobody could remember much afterwards. A great many people took offense at this fool. There was only one person who could begin to explain it. A very respected man looked down at a child and said, "Do you really think it is right to laugh so much after what happened to her?" And then, for just a moment, the child said, "He understood that. But if we really understood, laughter wouldn't be enough."

There were other things that he did that offended people, and those he offended sought to drive him away. And he returned to his home, the palace of the Fairy Queen.

But he had not really left. The fairy prince's kiss was no ordinary kiss. It was a magic kiss. When he kissed you, he gave his spirit, his magic, his fairy blood. And the world looks very different when there is fairy blood coursing through your veins. You share the fairy prince's kiss, and you can pass it on. And that pebble left behind an ever-expanding wave: we have magic, and wonder, and something deeper than either magic or wonder.

And that is how universe was re-enchanted.

Adam looked down at his daughter and said, "There, Sweetie. Have I told the story the way you like it?"

The child said, "Yes, Daddy, you have," climbed into her father's lap, and held up her mouth for a kiss.

Epilogue

No one spoke after that.

Finally, after a time, Barbara said, "Can we go outside, Daddy? I bet the snow's real good now."

Father Basil said, "Why don't we all go out? Just a minute while I get my gloves. This is snowball making snow."

Five minutes later, people stepped out on the virgin snow. Macrina said, "This is wonderful. It's like a fairy wonderland."

Paul said, "No. It's much more wonderful than that."

Then the snowballs flew, until Adam said, "See if you can

hit that snowplough!"
> And then it was time to go home.